Between the Cracks
Interfering with stories

Also by A.R. McHugh

Saccades

The Tales of Cupid and Psyche

The Silver Bestiary

Between the Cracks

A.R McHugh

The right of A.R. McHugh to be identified as the author of this
work has been asserted in accordance with the Copyright Act 1968.
ISBN: 978-0-6489145-9-4
This edition published in Australia in 2022 by Diving Bell, an
imprint of Diving Bell Education. www.divingbelleducation.com

Cover image: Image is in the public domain.

For my father, who believes that there are many ways of telling a story

Contents

Labyrinth

There are, however, other stories also about marriages of Theseus which were neither honorable in their beginnings nor fortunate in their endings, but these have not been dramatized.

Plutarch, *Life of Theseus*

They had expected it to be terrifying; blood from previous sacrifices all over the gates and the sound of snorting from deep within. In fact, there were no gates and the whole place was green and quiet as a sacred grove – which, in a way, it was.

Theseus had decided that he would be leaving Crete alive, with or without the king's pretty daughter, and that none of Minos' mind-games would bother him. Minos was considerably less frightening than the prospect of going back to Athens with nothing more to show for the adventure than his own sorry hide. The belief that he was a hero, and so had to do heroic things, governed Theseus' every interaction. If there was no possibility of heroism, he would ferret about the place, riling up kings and lower creatures, until he discovered one.

He wasn't hopeful about the maze as a locus of heroic deeds – it looked much too pretty in the afternoon sunlight, and the Minotaur was much too quiet to be a real challenge. But the group of snivelling, vomiting teenagers behind him made him keen to put on a good show. The greater he made the trepidation, he reasoned, the greater would be his achievement in overcoming whatever lay within.

'I'll go first,' he said, drawing his sword. The understanding reached with Minos had been that every member of the Athenian tribute party had a full day to escape the Minotaur. At sunrise, when they had not recrossed the gate – and no one ever had – they would be replaced by another tribute.

Thick, scratchy hedges had been planted before the walls of the maze, so the impression was of a stroll down a lane, unless you parted

11

the leaves and found the marble behind them. He spent about an hour taking left turns, which took him further into the maze than he would have thought possible. It had looked small, or rather, smaller than this, when he had walked around the outside of the maze the previous evening with Ariadne, her damp hand clutching his arm. He laughed at this needlessly complex way of asserting Crete's dominance over Athens. And the thought of Ariadne, who had given him the ball of twine behind her father's back, with a look of deep, green-eyed promise.

That reminded him, he thought. He tied one end to a branch and kept walking.

The sun arced overhead and he stopped for water. He realized he was footsore and had been walking for over two hours. He was beginning to feel faintly queasy from all the turning. Irritably, he kicked at a hedge and his foot met the marble behind it. He calmed himself, realizing that wall-kicking was unheroic, and that marble walls indicated a challenge worthy of him.

Reassured he pressed on, wandering from green lane to green lane, trying not to make any conscious choices, but rather to put himself in the hand of the goddess who had always directed his destiny. The beast, he thought, would present itself to him, be dispatched, and become another monument in the Sacred Way of his own legend.

Turning and turning in the deepening twilight, he thought about Ariadne's eyes, and the pulse that had drummed in her as she closed his fingers around the ball of twine. He imagined how he would wind the twine around her and take her home to Athens where she would embellish his home. The home he would have, he corrected himself, when his name was known beyond the Middle Sea and enemies quaked when his sandals trod the dust of their ignominious little kingdoms. Corinth, Argos, Mycenae.

He must have slept, because he woke to moonlight and cold, and a dead silence that infuriated him. He *must* be near the centre. The twine had long since run out and he saw small, stepped structures in the corners of the maze's infinite courtyards. He called down many curses and ugly on the Minotaur, then on Pasiphae the whore, and finally on Minos and his strumpet daughter who were in all respects unworthy of him.

Exhausted and aching from cold and anticipation, he finally heard a laboured wheeze, as of the breathing of a great beast. Thanking the goddess and trying not to feel angry about how long it had taken her, Theseus tossed back his curls and settled his cloak on his shoulder, where it would protect his left bicep and look appropriately manly.

He saw himself as he knew legend would later see him; sword bared and muscular thigh advancing to meet the half-bull son of Minos' shame. The wheeze increased and he tried to get a fix on its position, flattening himself against the freezing wall. He was afraid of blood, and longed for the sword to encounter some fleshy foundation on which he could build his name.

He inched into the central circular space at the labyrinth's heart. Alone beneath a vast grey moon, he saw an immense disk of polished silver, framed by a pair of bull's horns. His own laboured breathing rattled off it, rebounded around the space and echoed as a bovine wheeze.

Between the horns he saw a teenage boy, acne-speckled and knobby-jointed, an Adam's apple sticking out like a boll on a tree trunk. Theseus the useless, the bastard, whom Athens had cast adrift as a mouth unworthy to feed.

He stared long at the image, before running upon his sword. His blood was black as a bull's in the moonlight.

Alkestis

Some corpse or other had to be delivered to the underworld…
Euripides, *Alkestis*

So I died instead of him; Admetus I mean – my husband.

We were watching the children run figure eights around the orange trees he had planted when he brought me from Iolcus. Halfway around, Eumelus changed direction and collided with Perimele. They fell over and started squalling. We went to them and picked up one each. I caught my daughter's scent on the breeze – heat, child-sweat and myrtle from her last hair wash – and the world darkened. I turned to Admetus and said, 'It's here.'

To his credit, he knew exactly what I meant. We put the children down and went into the house, gripping hands and forcing ourselves to walk slowly. Five years before, Apollo had announced this last and greatest boon to Admetus – that he'd talked the Fates into accepting a substitute for Admetus' death, if a volunteer could be found. H did it at dinner, so the entire household heard. But there was no point in alarming everyone now that it had come. It might take months. Years, if we were lucky.

We were unlucky. That's a stupid figure of speech, because if the whole thing has proven anything, it's that luck has nothing to do with it.

It took me two full days to die, and it was only Admetus' utter gutlessness that made me believe him when he swore not to remarry. He was afraid I'd return as a shade and haunt his bed.

Dying for two days and dead for one, and I can't remember what any of it felt like. Like childbirth, women – wives, not that there's any difference in Greek – forget the pain of dying so that we can do it over and over again for the cowards we've married.

I became aware of the roof of the tomb just as the torches went out. There was a long moment of sputtering sounds in the darkness and I realized where I was. I thought that it was the first time in in my entire life that I'd been completely alone. If I could have wriggled with contentment in my shroud I would have. It really was immensely satisfying to have completed life's greatest hurdle and now to be enjoying some peace and quiet in the voiceless, undemanding dark. I even found that the hangnail of Admetus' cowardice had ceased to nag me, and he was like a distant bout of the cold – a memory which provoked no sensations at all.

I tried not to think about the children.

Time has no meaning when you're dead. You experience no change and you cannot control your thoughts or your memories, but they tell me that I was only in the tomb for a single day before that interfering halfwit brought me back. Not that I'd gone anywhere. There was a kind of glow in the dark, like a lantern covered over with dark cloth and he came gradually into my tomb. Thanatos, that is, whose hand I grasped of my own volition.

Now that I'm back in the world of men and being talked to again as if I'm an idiot, they tell me that he has many guises, and that whatever I saw was a palliative for my poor befuddled female brain. I just look past them and maintain my silence, and know that they fear death and they fear me.

But he chose well, Thanatos, if he designed his appearance to comfort me. I saw the glow, even though my eyes had begun to harden and cover with a milky glaze of blindness. He came closer and I saw a tall man, neither young nor old, with a single sweep of shining black hair across his brow and black eyes. I had the sense of being properly looked at for the first time and I suddenly thought that death wouldn't be so bad. No children, no childbearing, no husband. I recognized possibilities for myself alone which had never been before.

He held out his hand to me. No man had ever held my hand without some other man first giving it to him. I had been like a baton handed from runner to runner, all fleeing something.

I don't know what happens if you refuse Thanatos' hand. He looked strong; maybe you're dragged away. But he was handsome, so maybe it's just a ploy to make you want to go. I don't care – it was just nice that for once my wishes were considered. I put my hand in his. It was cool and dry and not what you'd expect Death to feel like. I wondered if his lips were the same and I saw him give the faintest twist of a smile. With the brain dying, I suppose our thoughts must exist somewhere outside of ourselves. I assure you too, that even the dead can blush.

Our hands had no sooner touched than there was a grinding sound and a shaft of afternoon sun hit the tomb floor like a javelin. Thanatos' hand closed around mine and he drew me tight against him. Briefly I thought it was pleasant to feel the cool, solid strength of him, but then a part of me sighed and realized that I was again no more than a counter for boys to squabble over. I thought about running to some third place – but where is there that Death can't find you? And running in a shroud makes the universe look as absurd as it really is.

I won't bore you with the struggle between Thanatos and Heracles. That's who it was, incidentally. I guessed as much from the sheer thick brawn of him and the fact that everything he said was monosyllabic. There was an excess of manliness and when they had each other in a complicated torque hold, Thanatos suddenly struck the ground twice in defeat, and vanished.

It only occurred to me much later that Apollo had probably worked it out this way. It made me wonder just how much of a friend to my husband he had ever been. After all, Admetus fled Death like a snivelling child when he knew I would take his place, but once I was gone he realized that he would have to live with his own cowardice and his family's revulsion. And although he got me back, he has to live with my mute disgust too. What sort of friend does that to you?

16

The idea that I'd rather stay with Thanatos didn't occur to Heracles. (It didn't occur to Thanatos either, but I know I'll see him again at some point). Not much did. Walking *and* talking was an effort for him, so the whole way back from the tomb he concentrated on swinging his club at stones and pulling his lionskin on and off his head. We stopped to rest and the milky haze lifted from my eyes and he said, 'Do you think I can count that as one of my labours?' I was so annoyed that I didn't bother answering, and he took it as evidence that I was still consecrated to death – as if I hadn't been for the last five years.

He led me back to Pherae and handed me over, still veiled, to Admetus who, to my satisfaction, looked terrible. Admetus argued that he couldn't accept a strange woman into his home when he'd promised me that he wouldn't. That lasted five minutes, until he realized who I was. Heracles said that my silence would end on the third day out of the tomb, then picked up his club and left, humming like a simpleton.

It has been over a thousand days and I have not uttered a sound. I'm entitled to. I died for my husband and now it seems I must live for him too. A long slow rage keeps me going, a rage at my lot, at Apollo's ignorance of what my life would be, thus dragged from life to death and back again. Even when I'm cold and tired and would seek Admetus' arms the old disgust at his cowardice rises up and I gag on it. Apollo may have talked the Fates into letting Admetus off, but not me. I concentrate now on making our house his tomb, and our marriage a cold, constricting, inescapable shroud.

Daphne

Phoebus hopes for what he desires, but his own oracular powers fail him.
Ovid, *Metamorphoses*

It begins, like so many things, in a quarrel between brothers. Two boys, of golden good looks, with the slim strong bodies of the divinely youthful. They are Speed, Sunlight, Proportion, and Desire, Pursuit, and Passion respectively. And they're about to have a sibling slapping match.

'What're you doing with that?' Apollo gestures to the bow and arrows in Cupid's hands. '*I'm* archery. Get your own thing.'

But Cupid just laughs and twangs the bowstring to annoy his brother. Neither is sure who is the elder – aeons will pass and we'll still be arguing about which came first, the principle of attraction which is Cupid's domain, or the elements fused together by it, which is Apollo's.

'You're not the only one who enjoys huntin', shootin', and fishin',' says Cupid lazily. 'It's probably more my line anyway.'

Apollo grabs the quiver strap slung across Cupid's broad chest and yanks his brother towards him. 'There's not a thing alive that won't yield to my arrows. Let's get this absolutely clear. *I'm* the archer, not you – you glorified pander.'

Breathing in his brother's cool, divine breath with its perfume of prophecy, Cupid shoves him off. 'You might pierce everything with your arrows, but mine'll pierce *you*.'

Apollo smirks. 'Bring it, squirt. At least I can do something about it.' He casts a scornful eye at Cupid's nether-regions, which remain innocent of the raging desire he provokes in others. It annoys Cupid, to be unable to enjoy passion, but until now he had believed no one knew how much it annoyed him.

'Whatever. Just wait, golden boy. You'll feel a prick and it'll be all over. Think of me when you're in agony over some girl.' Cupid blows his brother a saucy kiss and flies off. Apollo swears and spits after him. He has almost forgotten the whole thing when, later in the day (if days mean anything at the beginning of time), he feels a sharp pain which has somehow eluded his divine foresight.

It's hard to grasp just *how much* the gods believe they're invincible. It makes you wonder why they get so angry, so jealous, about the things that we do down here. If nothing can harm them, why care? In fact, it tells you something about them: nothing they do makes sense, and they mostly have the emotions of children. Since they don't live in this world, they have no reason to grow up.

With the craftiness typical of a god, Cupid doesn't mention that his arrows are somewhat different to Apollo's. They come in two kinds: one provokes desires, like the scratch that triggers some horrible infection; the other makes its victim flee any kind of desire. This is the power that you don't think of – that the object of your obsession will feel an equal and opposite emotion, will flee just as hard as you chase, feel as much disgust as you feel desire. Actually, it's worse: they'll feel disgust *because* you feel desire. It's like walking a badly-trained dog: the harder you pull them to you, the harder they pull away, until the two of you are wheezing and fighting up the street, the laughing-stock of everyone. This is the real sting in Cupid's quiver. Apollo's in charge of the sun: its comings and goings, arc and eclipse, how hot it burns, how splendidly it sets. He's not afraid of a bit of heat. But he doesn't know, he can't even conceive of the idea that when he fixes his divine eye on some girl, she won't be thrilled to bits. So when he feels the prick of his brother's arrow, he shouts a few insults, and then ignores it.

Now look downwards, down from the ether and diaphanous cloud-drifts, where the air thickens and becomes moist with the breath of millions of lower, living things, the gods' marvellous toys. In a forest is a girl, doing nothing in particular. Just being in the forest, quiet and happy to be smaller than this great girdling world of green and dark.

This, as you've guessed, is Daphne. Right now Daphne is lying on the riverbank, trailing a hand in the water, wondering if she could guddle a fish. Her skirt is hiked up. There's mud on her knees and ankles and her feet are, frankly, unspeakable. Fifteen years of skipping about barefoot in the forest will do that. There are probably things living in her hair, which sits in a messy ponytail. But she's brown, fit, young, and happy just being on her own.

To Cupid, still looking for a way to pay back his golden brother, it's irresistible. Daphne doesn't even feel the prick of the arrow, which will make her run like a hare from Apollo, who's been shot with one of the other kind.

It doesn't enter Daphne's messy head that anyone would come bothering her about love, let alone the god who drives the sun into the sky. She has an agreement with her father, poor old Peneus, who had wanted a normal daughter, and a nice son-in-law, and a couple of grandkids who didn't cry too much.

'Come on,' he said to her, trying not to sound wheedling. 'You *owe* me a wedding. A son-in-law. Kids. You can choose! I'm not going to saddle you with someone you don't like. I'm just asking you to get on and pick…well, *anyone* at this stage.'

Daphne asked for more time. Then she cried. Then she raged. Then she sulked. She shut herself in her room, went off to the forest for days, and was rude to the bewildered boys who came with their parents and sat, smiling, on the edge of the couches as Daphne put a frog in their wine, ate with her mouth open, or picked her nose at the table. Eventually her father gave up. No, she doesn't have to marry. Yes, she can go to the forest. He won't keep harping on about grandchildren. He promises.

Mothers, fathers – they'll tell you anything. Promises, assurances, guarantees, all of which the world treats as dust and words. It grinds on, sucking in and crushing like oranges all those surprised, resentful children. The world ignores your parents' promises. It's what the world does. And parents still make them, because it's what parents do.

But Daphne doesn't have time to think of all this when she looks up from the clear ripples, always changing and always the same, like all streams. Her glance falls on a pair of sandalled feet on the other side of the river. Nice feet, going up to nice ankles, well-turned calves, strong straight knees, then a fine linen tunic which shows a well-developed chest and archer's arms. And the face. It's like a line-and-point primer for draughtsmen, showing proportion, evenness, grace, long golden brows and blue eyes, as startled by the muddy girl on the other bank as she is by him.

Then, like the sudden clap of a bird's winds in the noon silence, all the poison of Cupid's arrows is released into their respective systems. Her throat tightens; his eyes widen; a huge surge of speed and panic slams through them both. She's up and running away, away to anywhere safe, whatever that looks like.

But he's running too: he's just seen the thing which is to him what the sun is to the rest of us. Not since the Titans emerged from the chaos of atoms and made the world has a god been this astonished, this desirous to possess something.

Apollo doesn't think – he *can't* think – that this is all due to the sharp pain he felt an hour ago. He's too busy running after her, into the trees where she's always been so safe, so happy.

'Stop!' Even he realizes that it's futile to shout this when someone has decided to sprint *away* from you. This is one of love's indignities – you stop making sense. 'Stop! It's me! Apollo!'

His voice disappears among the silent trees. 'God of the sun! The archer, the hunter – so there's no need to run.' *Stupid*, he thinks, *that sounds like a threat.* 'I didn't mean I'm hunting you – I mean, just…stop running!'

Still nothing. Why would a girl flee, actually *run away from* a god? And a good-looking god at that, he thinks. It's not as if he's Mars or Vulcan, all sweaty and threatening.

'I can give you music! Dancing, poetry, prophecy,' he shouts, starting to jog onwards again. *Why is she hiding*, he thinks irritably. *I want to love her. That amazing face! Those ankles and sweet little feet.* A snake skitters away from his foot and he skips to the side, stifling an ungodly squeal. 'Come on! I just want to get to know you! What's your name?'

With his divine hearing he detects her frantic heart, drumming like a rainstorm in her untouched chest. Then he's off again, covering leagues with his divine speed. But fear gives her the edge, for a while at least. Imagine that, how frightened you'd have to be to outrun a *god*. That's the effect of Cupid's other arrows, the ones you never hear about. Sick with fear, she runs as if she's flying. She couldn't have told you why she's running. Like Apollo, Daphne's now in a state beyond rational thought. Her instincts have been replaced by a lamb's – and Apollo is the wolf.

But humans are laughably fragile, compared to those higher forces. Like a paper kite in a rainstorm, we simply can't last at that pitch. You might as well try to scramble out of a black hole. He's gaining on her, still calling stupid stuff, but he can afford to shout and run at the same time because he's divine and she's tiring. She sobs and pants. All she wants to do is destroy her own beauty, the way you scribble out something you've written in anger, the way a fugitive wants to destroy their own scent.

She feels him enter her airspace, feels his heat at her back, his forefoot skipping against her heel. She does the only thing you can do, which is usually useless. With her last breath she shouts out to her father. 'You promised!'

She doesn't expect much to come of it. It's more a cry of rage against an unfair world. But we tell *this* story and none of the others where cries of anger have absolutely no effect, because this time someone hears her.

Apollo puts an arresting hand on Daphne's heaving shoulder, but it's too late. The metamorphosis has begun. A huge heaviness washes through Daphne, like warm oil slipping along her joints. Blurrily she looks at her feet and sees her toes browning like hazelnuts, extending rootlets into the earth. An embracing feeling, like a firm bandage, is creeping up her legs, past her knees, her hips. All she wants is to yawn and stretch her arms overhead. An armour of bark, smooth and slightly silvery, is covering her, impervious to Apollo's scrabbles. Now he has inherited all her panic. She looks up at her hands; her fingertips are fluting, greening. She is becoming part of the world that she loved so much.

Before her, Apollo is ashen. He looks like a man about to lose his own life, if that's possible for a god. He kisses her armoured waist, her chest, feeling her heart, deep beneath the bark, still shuddering at his touch.

At last it is done. He slides down the trunk and slumps at the foot of the dainty tree, its boughs waving like a dancer with garlands. The slender leaves above him rustle and clap; Apollo sobs, and none of it can quite drown out the sound of Cupid's hard laughter.

Phaethon

The Sun, seated in the middle, looked at the boy, who was fearful of the strangeness of it all, with eyes that see everything...
     Ovid, *Metamorphoses*

As he falls, fiery and smoking, from the wrecked chariot, Phaethon's last thought is despairing. He wanted a tiny measure of control over his life, which he sees as an ember, summoned into being on a divine whim and now blown out because he has presumed upon his parentage. He understands now that he never had any control over anything. He strikes the surface of the river and is vapourized.

*

'That's cobblers,' Epaphus said, looking at Phaethon slyly. 'Your father's just Merops. Apollo – as if. Why can't you just admit you're ordinary? You're such a try-hard.' Huddled around Phaethon and his tormentor so that parents would not see or hear, the other boys sniggered and shuffled. There was no doubt that Zeus was Epaphus' father. His mother, Io, grazed peacefully in the meadow a stone's throw from her son's bullying.

Phaethon, tow-headed and snub-nosed, was an unlikely son of the Archer-God. If it wasn't that his mother, the Oceanid Clymene, sometimes surfaced to speak to him (when it was absolutely necessary), Phaethon wouldn't have believed it himself. As it was, she had mentioned it absently, before letting the waves cover her, and didn't reappear for months. Merops, his stepfather, confirmed it.

'It's true,' he said, putting a stroke on the top of a letter. He had recently given his people the gift of writing, of which he was rather proud. Phaethon noticed that Merops was always fiddling with something when they spoke to each other. He suspected it allowed him to avoid eye contact with his teenage stepson. 'But it happened a long time ago, and for all practical purposes, I'm your father.' His gaze flickered timidly to Phaethon. 'And we love you, son.'

For a moment Phaethon was afraid that Merops would squeeze his shoulder or give him a manly chest punch. He muttered something and left Merops to his alphabet. In the portico, Epaphus was talking to the others. 'Been chatting with your…father?' he called. There was a ripple of obedient laughter from Epaphus' lackeys.

Phaethon walked away, burning with the urge to say something. He went out of the city gate and took the eastern road, telling himself that he would walk until he stopped feeling angry and had a plan. He walked further east, then still further.

*

Like a wind blowing a fire's embers further than is really safe, Phaethon is blown by shame and anger towards the place where day begins. In his mind's eye Epaphus gestures and peacocks, and Phaethon cannot stop thirsting for that poise, the assurance, the deference, he tells himself bitterly, that comes with the acknowledgement of how damn special you are. Of your true paternity. Of any paternity except dusty, careful, fussy, boring Merops.

At some point he reaches it, the place of beginnings, without people or shadows. Without anything much, actually. Phaethon suspects he's close because space flattens into a long white plane and the smell of the world disappears into a clean, dry heat, like the smell of electricity. The place becomes increasingly dimensionless as Phaethon heads towards a brighter light. Brighter and brighter until he feels the skin of his closed eyelids begin to sizzle. He pastes his hands over his eyes and crawls towards the source. At some point he hears a voice saying something to another person about turning down the brightness.

He risks a peek.

There are thousands of bright figures assembled in ranks of ascending size around a glowing white orb. These, he realizes, are the ranks of time, which light makes meaningful to us. There are the seconds, all 86,400 of them, marshalled by the Hours, the Days, and Years. Phaethon can see little other than eyes which blink and float in the dazzling whiteness.

Then a voice from within the orb, says, 'What do you want?'

Phaethon should really have taken it as evidence that he's at least half-divine, if he can stand to hear that voice without his heart liquefying in his chest. But he's still fuming about Epaphus, so the fact that the orb is a god is less important than the fact that the orb is his father.

'I want my father.'

There's a silence and then some embarrassed shuffling. The gods' escapades with nymphs and mortal women are great light entertainment after dinner, but the results of those escapades don't usually come slogging up to the birthplace of Dawn demanding their dad.

'Phaethon?' It sounds as if even the gods can be caught off guard. 'Clymene's child?'

'And yours,' says Phaethon, stepping towards the burning orb. 'Father.'

The voice makes the right sort of paternal noises: *Nice you've come, aren't you tall, got any plans for the future?* Phaethon is about to write the whole thing off as more anodyne than Merops when Divine Dad says something about calling if he ever needs help. Anything at all. It's his.

'There is something,' says Phaethon.

'Anything, my son. You have my word.'

'Let me drive your chariot. Just once.'

There is another silence, different in quality to the last. Dismayed. 'Ask for something else. That's not…well, it's not *wise*.'

What's not wise, thinks Phaethon, *is dallying with a nymph and ending up with a mortal son who'll inevitably turn up at the wrong moment. That's what's unwise, Oh god of prophecy who needs to clean his spectacles-of-time.*

'A promise is a promise, father. I've never asked for anything – never even bothered you before now, and I never will after this.'

26

There is a sigh, the sound of someone getting up, and something being put aside. His eyes watering, Phaethon sees a hand set aside a diadem of rays from which the light emanates. A rather ordinary man in early middle age comes down from the steps of the throne-arrangement before now hidden by the light.

'Oh,' Apollo says. 'That's what you look like. Actually, you're a bit more like me than her.'

'Couldn't you see me before?' Phaethon is confused. All the fatherly chitchat before had sounded as though he was being looked over.

'Ah. No. Not really. It's the diadem, you see,' Apollo says, apologetically. 'Can't see past my own glory. Neither can anyone else. You're quite lucky – only my parents have actually seen me like this.'

'What about Mother?' says Phaethon, indignant.

'Oh no.' Apollo laughs. 'It's probably why I've got so many children. The mothers – all dazzled by the glory.'

'That's awful,' says Phaethon. 'I can't see why you're quibbling about the chariot when you go around…*dazzling* your way into women's company.'

Apollo sits on the steps and draws Phaethon down with him. 'I'm not quibbling. You don't know what you're asking. It's the task of a god – *my* task. My most important task, actually – to draw the sun into the sky. And that's just a figure of speech, to make it easier to understand what really goes on each morning. All the calibrations of the Earth's rotation, getting the sun at the right point every day so that it tallies with the seasonal apsis and doesn't scorch the life out of everything. Then there's the chariot and team – *not* my choice, believe me, but at the time it was the only way to get something that size moving. The horses scare me to bits. Four-footed lunatics. I've been doing this for 4.6 billion years and I'm only just getting the hang of it. Handling them, I mean. You couldn't possibly. You'd be killed. Worse – sorry, son, but this is true – you'd kill everyone else. No, look, ask for anything else and it'll be done in a trice. But that—' he sucks his teeth and shakes his head. Phaethon sees traces of Merops. It's obviously what happens when men become fathers, this adoption of a plumber's mannerisms.

'No. That's what I'm asking for. I'll be careful, I swear. But that's what I want.'

Apollo links his hands and hangs his head, thinking. After a minute he says, 'Right. Alright. But you must do exactly as I tell you. You might just get away with it if you're careful. And you keep your nerve.'

'I can do that,' says Phaethon, immediately. His earnestness makes Apollo quail inside.

So he takes Phaethon to the stables. Shows him the chariot, which is nearly three times higher than the boy. And the tream, which are more like dragons than horses. Rippling mains and tails of flame which stream from a central brightness, like Apollo's diadem. The snorting and stamping of equine fire, the red eyes which roll in the blurred-edge blazing heads, make Phaethon and Apollo skitter out of the way.

'They're used to my weight,' says Apollo. 'When I ride the chariot I assume my full divinity which is, as it were, hefty.'

'But it's about how you handle them, isn't it?' says Phaethon, who refuses to be talked out of this despite every cell veering away from the chariot in trepidation. A vision, more potent than the burning steeds, sits like a pair of borrowed spectacles between his eyes and the world. The chariot, driven by him in a glorious arc across the heavens, beneficently giving light to Epaphus and Merops and all the other dusty, disdainful doubters who will, naturally, eat their own hearts out with regret that they weren't nicer to him.

He hops into the chariot. Someone brings a box for him to stand on so that he can see over the rim. The trio is put in the traces. Dimly he hears Apollo telling him their names, telling him about the well-worn track he must follow across the sky, and the disasters which will result from deviating. He's too excited to listen. He's fingering the reins, feeling the team pull like magnets as he talks down the strap of gilded leather to them. He's driven Merops' chariot many times. Not the big one, the ceremonial one so heavy that it can only go slowly before the team tire and it becomes unstable. No, he's driven the everyday chariot – mid-weight, for a mid-weight team of biddable horses who are steadier than Phaethon will ever be.

And then it happens – the waters of Ocean part and the sun, like a gigantic bubble of lava, bounces gently up the launching ramp to the surface, its billions of nuclear explosions occurring every second, making the Pacific steam like a faulty cooling pond.

It's attached to the back end of the chariot. Phaethon, his semi-divine skin crinkling from the radiation, picks up the reins and pretends to be in control as one of his half-sisters leads the horses to the gates of Dawn. These open with a slow majesty which Phaethon feels in his mortal soul.

His father puts a hand on Phaethon's sweating arm.

'Ask anything else, son. But get down and let me do this.'

In the future, the Chariot could be used as a measure of pride, the way that the distance from Sun to Earth is used as an Astronomical Unit. One Chariot is 4.3 seconds, the measure of youthful male pride reckoned in the time between release and catastrophe.

This is the length of time that it takes for the horses to rip away from the grooms' hands, to begin the climb up the track to which Apollo keeps them every morning, to feel the absence of his weight from the chariot. And because they are horses of the highest, rarest breeding, they are also completely unstable, and begin veering delightfully wherever they want. Phaethon is thrown like an acorn from side to side, laying on the reins. But it's like a bee trying to control an eagle – the team barely feel the leather on their steaming backs.

Imagine it from far below: the glow of Dawn suddenly brightens. The ball of fire zips to and fro like a meteor, like a shooting star jumping, dotting about the sky. Then – terrifying, unbelievable – it zooms in, a close up of the Sun, which no one is left to see because they're ash and shadows from the corona alone. And just as suddenly, it's yanked back, the world plunged into darkness as the chariot drags it over to the other hemisphere and sears them like a judiciously-done steak, charred neatly on both sides.

Primitive people are boiled alive.

Zeus, smelling the delicious scent of a planet's worth of baked meats, looks over the top of his aegis and is furious. The pretty little things he has so recently placed on Earth, like painted figures in a diorama, are discoloured. Around the world's middle is a scar which no amount of polishing will remove, and the denizens are now black and swollen-featured. He looks with the eye of eternity, deep into their genetic futures and sees that this solar trauma will inhere forever. He makes a noise of disgust and picks up the dreaded bolt.

Of course, Zeus is equally aware of his grandson's blank terror, and Apollo's despair, and Epaphus sudden pain, and Merops' panic. Zeus knows all things at all times: he is equally present in this moment, and the moments before Phaethon's birth, and those long after, when the Earth is cold, dark, and unpeopled.

He is present in the thunderbolt which he raises and hurls, like a javelin, at his grandson.

Phaethon feels a tremendous force, shattering all the bones in his chest as the bolt strikes the chariot. It is only slightly more powerful than his fear.

He falls through the burning ozone. His dying brain recognizes that Epaphus was right: better to be ordinary, if this is where being special gets you.

He is a lump of half-roasted meat before he strikes the surface of the river Eridanus, sizzling like bacon fat. The stench is awful.

This is the world of fathers, gods, names: everything burning, a dead boy, and a bad smell.

The Gardener

All means should be tried first, but whatever is unresponsive to treatment should be pared away, lest the healthy part become infected too.
    Ovid, *Metamorphoses*

Miss Rhys said she would organize the memorial garden. There were other women in the village who would have enjoyed the protracted period of consultation, planning, and design, but the village felt that it was Miss Rhys's due, since she had taught the village children for nearly half a century (including the boys for whom the garden was a memorial), and because she could provide most of the plants from her own stock, thus costing Steeple Claydon almost nothing.

The space given over to the garden lay in the marshy ground behind the village square; it had been slated for development, but the cost of drainage proved prohibitive. Undaunted, Miss Rhys turned the marsh into a lake, incorporating the reeds and abundant amphibian life within her design. After a year of work, the garden was opened by the lord lieutenant of the county and his wife, a classicist of some minor fame who moonlighted as a telly-don. Officially named the Tom Underwood Memorial Garden, it commemorated a boy who had disappeared nearly half a century before and was commonly believed to have drowned in the mill race. The absence of a body led to darker whispers, as did the five other young men whose disappearance over a fifty-year span caused the village to mourn and ponder. All the boys had been hale, high-spirited young men, given to breaking windows and hearts, and who had not been above attempting to relieve village girls of their dignity in the marshy little copse which was now their memorial. Bodies had never been found, and the absorption of masterful young men into the world was eventually assumed to be the way of things. The garden which was

31

eventually made for them was known informally as the Lost Boys Park.

'Such beautiful plants,' said Dr Carruthers, the lord lieutenant's wife, coming up behind Miss Rhys. 'And a very peaceful design. Just right for sitting here meditating on time. *Forma bonum fragile est.* Poor boys. Did you know them well?'

Miss Rhys squinted at the woman, who was framed by the bunting brought out from the church hall for the opening. 'Oh yes,' she said. 'I taught them all as children. Tom Underdown was in my very first class when I came back to Steeple Claydon after university. They were all lively boys. Sometimes too lively, if you ask some of the women here.'

'Hasn't that always been the way with boys?' said Dr Carruthers fondly. 'They break our hearts and become our heroes.'

'Quite,' said Miss Rhys. 'I wondered if the plants meant anything to you, as a classicist, I mean.'

The telly-don stiffened slightly, feeling as if she were being tested. Her most popular programmes had been the racier ones. *Gladiators, Governors, and Gonads*, on Pompeii. *The Food of Love: Cooking the Classics*, and the BBC's Children in Need charity one-off: *Agrippina v Messalina: Rome's Biggest Bonk-Off.* She hadn't translated much more than a school motto for years. 'I'm not entirely...'

'From the *Metamorphoses*,' said Miss Rhys, dead-heading a ranuncula.

Dr Carruthers looked at the garden, searching for some deeper allusion in the tweedy arrangement of boring greenery and sapling trees. She was planning a special on Gardens of Greece, but it was being held up by the Beeb's unwillingness to pay for an entire crew to spend the summer in the Greek Islands. She noticed a lot of bay laurels, which everyone remembered as the tree into which poor old Daphne had been transformed as she fled Apollo's advances. 'Oh yes,' she said. 'The laurels. That's a nice gesture. I suppose we do see our young men as Apollonian types. Chasing loathly maidens and all.

Witty.' She tried to resist a curl of her lip at the village schoolteacher's presumption that she could out-reference a telly-don. At a loss, she took herself off to the lakeside and sat on a bench (the gift of the county sexual assault hotline), while Miss Rhys manned the tea urn.

Dr Carruthers had been sitting on the bench for a while, politely receiving, and then impatiently fending off, requests for autographs when she noticed an avenue of saplings running either side of the path which led to the lake. She recognized the young trees as poplars, alternating the black variety with the white. It dredged up an undergraduate memory. Weren't black poplars the metamorphosis of Dryope, the poor little wood nymph who was raped by Apollo? And Leuke, another nymph equally badly treated by Hades - she was turned into a white poplar. Perhaps the schoolmarm wasn't so unsubtle after all.

The lake was a pretty oval of blue-gray, reflecting the gentle clouds and English summer sky. Reeds softened the edges; emerging from them into the deeper waters was a statue of a young girl, slender-bodied and maidenly. A breeze whispered through the reeds.

'Nice, innit,' said a woman at her elbow. She balanced a selection of cakes on a large paper plate.

'It's lovely,' said Dr Carruthers, thoughtfully. 'A nice memorial.'

'Not that some of them deserved it,' said the woman, biting into a mound of scone and cream. 'When I was a girl this was just marsh and scrubby bushes. I caught young Billy Carew coming out of them one night like a rabbit. And the Garner girl, she who's Mrs Thomas Atkins now—,' she gestured with a dimpled elbow to a family group with a round blonde woman in the centre, her arm around a round blonde child, a peaceful smile on her straw-hat-shaded face. 'She was in a terrible state. It weren't no sorrow at all that Billy Carew vanished. And he don't deserve no garden neither. But it's nice, all the same.' She ambled off towards the tea tent.

The reeds whispered *Syrinx, Syrinx*, thought the telly-don. Syrinx, who had been raped by Pan, and called upon her sisters in her plight, was turned into a reed forever whispering her own name. She looked around the memorial garden, whose careful planning reflected Miss Rhys's delicate arbitrating mind. God, it said in a very English way, was a gardener. She identified heliotrope, with a cloud of butterflies like a purple nimbus - the transformation of Clytie, abandoned by Helios. And around the rocks near the trestle tables, little psalakanthos, the metamorphosis of a girl bullied to death by Dionysus. She saw a walnut tree sapling, which would offer shade to future villagers and whisper the story of Karya, another of Dionysus' maidenly victims. She saw Miss Rhys, standing pale and enigmatic in the shade of a small pine tree, and recognized an arboreal allusion to Pitys, who fled the violence of Pan.

She walked back to the centre of the garden, where her husband was making conversation with the vicar. Around an oak sapling the ladies of Steeple Claydon played with their children, admired the roses, kissed their husbands, and waved to each other across the design drawn by Miss Rhys's fruitful, law-giving hand. She looked at the oak. Erysichthon cut down an oak sacred to Demeter, she remembered, killing the dryad nymph within it in the process. An abominable crime, this assertion of masculine violence over the gentle, mighty prerogatives of female nature. A discreet bronze plaque, on a tasteful piece of sandstone, bore a few lines. *Cuncta prius temptanda sed inmedicabile curae, ense recidendum ne pars sincera trahatur.* She struggled for a few minutes with the passive subjunctive of *traho, trahere* and finally recognized it from Ovid. *All means should be tried first, but whatever is unresponsive to treatment should be pared away, lest the healthy part become infected too.*

The memory of the young men who had violated Steeple Claydon's slow and orderly passage through the centuries remained in the garden, commuted to a vegetal form that would be firmly and continually pruned back. Dr Carruthers felt a creeping sensation that she dimly recognized as humility.

'It'll be very beautiful in the future,' said Miss Rhys, relieved of her duty at the tea-urn. She handed the telly-don a cup and saucer. The telly-don took it carefully, and noticed her husband making his familiar *time-to-go* signal. She had a meeting with her editor to go over the rushes of her next programme, which debated the proposition of women's lib in the ancient world. Miss Rhys caught the exchange and smiled briefly. The telly-don drank her tea obediently, watching the retired teacher over the cup's rim. Miss Rhys reminded her of a pair of garden shears - sharp, accurate, and lethal to the careless.

House and Garden

But the Lord God called to the man, 'Where are you?'
Book of Genesis 3:8

My responsibility was to tend to the garden. The plants and the trees provided all the food that we needed. Then the Boss created birds and animals from the dust of the ground, and delegated to me the job of naming them like an evaluation on which my end-of-year bonus depended.

Though the animals and birds were beautiful, it was definitely a bit on the lonely side.

I sent something to that effect through to the Boss, who arranged for a period of leave (leave-of-consciousness, that is). When I woke up there was another quite like me with a note stuck on it saying *Female: for you.* And my side hurt a bit.

All in all Female-for-you and I and the Boss got along swimmingly. We all dwelt in the Garden quite happily and got along with our jobs in a decent fashion. I should point out that there were two trees in the Garden. The Tree of Life, and the Tree of the Knowledge of Good and Evil.

The Boss told me, and I told Female-for-you to stay away from the latter. He was quite explicit that to eat of that tree would bring death.

What transpired I only put together later, when it was all too late. One day, when Female-for-you was alone, she happened upon a serpent in the Tree of the Knowledge of Good and Evil. The Serpent asked her what the Boss had said about the tree. Female-for-you said that He had warned us that we would die pursuant to our eating from the tree.

The serpent told Eve, fairly briskly, that this was either a lie or a memo read out of context. He further told her, that if she and I ate of

36

the tree we'd actually circumvent the org chart and go to the top of the tree.

Female-for-you exercised some initiative, ate from the tree and then gave me some fruit too. Since she was in charge of supply and logistics, I didn't question this (not wishing to intrude on her designated role) and only became aware that something was amiss some time later.

I suddenly became aware of an unpleasant coolness in my nether regions. I had never noticed these before, not in all their sharp detail. Until that day they had been rather fuzzy, as though when looking south of my chest my eyes became short-sighted. I realised, with a sickening kind of intuition, that I was naked. And so was Female-for-you.

Things moved swiftly after that. We heard footsteps. Immediately, Female-for-you bolted beneath a bush, leaving me to hide behind the potting shed.

Soon, the Boss's voice rang out in the cool evening air.

I stammered nervously that we would really rather stay where we were, not being disposed to company that evening. When he asked why there was a long silence. I could see Female-for-you's eyes anxiously peering out from a frond. I wasn't going to answer. She gave a sigh. 'Because we're naked,' she said firmly.

I'll give the Boss this – he never minces his words, and he's swift to a conclusion. 'Did you eat from the tree that I told you not to eat from?'

I said hastily, 'The Female-for-you gave me the fruit and I took it and ate it.' I hoped he'd read between the lines and see that I hadn't initiated the chain of events.

Female-for-you narrowed her eyes and gave me a withering look. Then she blamed the serpent.

The Boss was fairly summary. He cursed the serpent, cursed me, cursed her, the tree, the potting shed, and everything else between the garden walls. An unheard-of amount of bad language was used.

A large gentleman appeared, turned us out of the Garden and advised us to go out and connurbate.

I remembered something I had left in the top left-hand drawer of the potting shed and asked if I could get it, but had a flaming sword waved meaningfully in my face. 'Just leaving,' I said, hurriedly and sat down on the pile of rubble which it has been my privilege to nurture since then.

Female-for-you, who has since changed her name by deed poll to 'Eve', gave a large sigh and said, 'Well, thank goodness for that. I can do subordination or laundry, not both. Things are going to be different from now on.'

I tried to remind her of what the Boss had said about her being subject to me and our offspring crushing the serpent. She gave me a prod. 'There are directives, and then there's the situation on the ground, of which the Boss is richly unaware. I'm outsourcing the subjection – get a dog if you want something to order around. And as for offspring, we have to mark out a quarter-acre here and space for a three-car garage. Get going.'

Promise

I have set my rainbow in the clouds, and it will be the sign of the covenant between me and the earth.
   Genesis 9:13

The air was still clearing when the clouds began to part and a weak sun shone through. Sitting exhausted on the sodden ground, watching the animals stream down the gangway beside the man who had saved them, Noah felt a characteristic rumbling inside his skull. There was a pressure between his eyes just above the bridge of his nose and he knew that after many months of rain and silence, the Lord was going to speak again. He quailed. This was never good, as the years-long inundation which rewound Creation itself back to watery chaos, had shown.

And so it came. That flat, humourless, nasal voice, speaking inside his head without the let or hindrance of air, vocal chords, or a break. Before the Flood, He had made a lengthy complaint about everything man had done. Now He told Noah How Things Were Going to Be.

If possible, it was worse. Animals would live in terror of man, whose task was simply to breed, like locusts. Everything that moved was there for food – except its blood. Blood could not be eaten; man's blood could not be shed in anger, though in retribution was fine; accounting for blood would be held at some unspecified endpoint. The voice talked on about blood, blood, blood. Noah thought, *He's got worse.* The long months of darkness and water had sent the Lord insane. Now He was obsessed with blood and multiplying. Noah closed his eyes. It was like sleep, he thought. A weird half-sodden world of two elements and a feeling of immense fear.

Look, said the voice. Noah looked about him. The animals had spread out a bit as the waters receded, browsing for grass in the mud.

Used to the single colour of deep, omnipresent water, the earth's muted solidity was reassuringly gentle, like eating toast after a violent gastric bug.

I establish my covenant with you. The light was growing harder, brighter. Noah's flood-weakened eyes watered at a shaft of sunlight, breaking and bending, vibrating and moving like a fish in the air. He cried out in terror. Far above him, on the deck of the ark, his wife and daughters-in-law were beginning the long task of shovelling the manure of ten thousand animals onto semi-dry land. They turned, saw the irradiated sky, and flung themselves face down.

This is my bow. Whenever I bring clouds over the earth and my bow appears, I will remember my covenant, between you and all living creatures of every kind.

Noah longed for the darkness and the peaceful flood. He did not know what a covenant was, or how long it would last. They had gone from one nightmare to another. Now they were doomed to live, generation after generation, beneath a sky on which a giant, capricious lunatic wrote his wishes.

Trickster

Laban, whose name means 'white'

Rachel looked like a candle flame, even in her sleep. Outside, a single tent away, I could hear Leah, my first wife, being sick. She was carrying our third child – even as I strove to give Rachel her first.

I gazed at Rachel and thought that there would never be a time when I was not thirsty for her. When her father told me that seven years had passed and that I finally had the right to take his second daughter as well as his first, a small voice within me panicked. For years I have been insatiable in the face of this woman. I have seen her at the well, in the sheep pens, at fields' edges, in twilight, at noon, in the snows, beneath the burning sun. I only need to see her outline from far off and my heart beats faster. Sometimes I think she is a test from the Lord my father's God. Sometimes I even care about passing that test.

I have watched her age and begin to show a tracery of those lines which surprise you underneath the face you believe you'll always wear. I have never ceased to desire her, right to the sharpest point of my very being. I feared that, when the fold of a marital tent finally dropped on us, there would be no more than silence and empty air, and the awkwardness of a brother- and sister-in-law who were now husband and wife.

They had darkened her eyes with kohl and covered her hair with a red veil. She made a kind of clutching, beckoning movement with her hand as if she was closing the years we had waited, crumpling them like an old leaf. I looked at her decorated palm, her pale wrist. My mouth met hers and we drowned the lost years.

Rachel woke and we lay together in our marriage bed and talked quietly until it seemed right to get up, show the bloodied sheet outside and get on with being the husband of two sisters.

Laban embraced me. 'Don't forget Leah,' he said in my ear. 'She's alone now.' I thought *And whose fault was that?*

Laban cheated me. But that is not the end. Nothing which results from a trick ever ends. I know, I've pulled off enough of them. Deception is a kink in the thread of events; it follows you, popping up again and again, sometimes like a joke, most times like a nightmare.

Perhaps this is why I loved Rachel and Leah. From a father so crooked, to a husband equally so, they remain as straight as peeled poplar rods. In my worst moments – after my first wedding night, for example, when I turned to see my wife in the early light, expecting Rachel's sleeping face and finding instead Leah's – I have wondered what it would take to ruin their sweet honesty. I thought about getting my revenge on Laban for tricking me with the wrong daughter by making her as crooked as he was. But I left it. Dug in for the long haul and waited until he would let me have Rachel too.

Oath

...he was an ignoramus, unlettered in the Law; like a sycamore shoot that is easily broken...

Genesis Rabbah on Judges 11

He hadn't realised that mud walls smoked as they burned. The last rider, on a beautiful pale horse of a kind he had never seen before, had thrown a brand through the doorway, catching his wife's loom. Tongues of flame ran nimbly up the warp and through the weft, seized the straw in the roof and carried away their home like so many djinn.

His wife watched stoically. This was the fourth house in their fifteen years of marriage that had been fired by the Ammonites. At least it was early in the summer. They could rebuild by autumn.

'You just stand there!' He was ranting at no one in particular.

She wanted the house to cool so that she could retrieve her loom weights. Forty little stones with holes bored in the centre for drawing the warp down, heavy and taut enough to work the shuttle through. Loom weights were all her mother had left her. They clicked and turned on the thread the way her mother's joints had clicked and ground in her thin skin. She half-wished the Ammonites would overrun them. What good had being the Chosen People actually done them? The only thing more permanent than her loom weights was the Living God's persistent, crotchety displeasure with them. She vaguely recalled something about an Ammonite god called Molech. She wondered if he was as difficult as theirs.

'What else am I going to do?' she said, neutrally.

'This is the fourth time. The fourth!'

She turned to him. 'And? Should I get like you? Ranting and tearing my hair, wearing sackcloth and all that grubby stuff? Will it stop it from having happened? Will it stop it from happening again?'

He was turning a slow puce. 'No, but ...'.

She turned on her heel. Maybe someone would have a tent they could use until they were housed again. Behind her, he was winding up to rail at the Lord again. 'Why do You visit this upon us? Why do the sins of others fall like a plague at our door? What have we, in this village, in the face of the ancient enemy, idolators and incestuous wretches all of them, done for You to reveal Your displeasure to us? Show us, Mighty One, where we have erred! Reveal to us the pattern of Your ways and we will sow in that pattern!'

She wandered away from him, pulling her veil over her head against the sun. A stillness crept over her as she put distance and silence between herself and the village. The flock, just beginning to regroup after scattering in terror, were speckles of white on the brown hills. She would gather them and drive them back to the village.

He wasn't a bad man, she thought, nor a bad husband. Just...wordy. Everything was met with a torrent of words, usually to the Lord, but whoever else was around got co-opted into the conversation. Sometimes she longed for the day he realised the Lord wasn't listening. What with the might of empires to control, other gods to fend off, nosey parkers who abominated His name and defiled His covenant – why would He bother with a lousy, dirt-poor village of dusty nobodies with only some scorched pots and a bag of heirloom stones to their name?

She hiked up her skirt, climbing the first foothill. They had sent the children, especially the girls, to the caves when the shepherds came flying down the road warning of riders. She scanned the brown undulations around, but saw nothing.

She plodded on. Her husband puzzled her – how could he be so oblivious to the sheer disinterest of heaven? She didn't believe the Lord was actively bad, despite the breath-taking pain of four labours and the daily humiliations of being in a body, and a female body at that. No one who created sunsets and figs, babies' toes and honey, the satisfaction in a tight, even weave, the delight in little hands waving a timbrel, could be actively bad. He was busy. He was a father to his people, and fathers were always busy. Her husband was just the demanding child of the family, always calling for attention, wanting an audience for his outrage, needing to know that other eyes saw him to assure him that he existed. He just had to be borne with and loved for who he was.

At least, she thought, going back down the slope with bent knees, he was handy. The goats fell into a messy, bony-rumped square before her, allowing themselves to be herded back to the village. She wished it were this easy to herd her husband. She realised that he was now effectively the headman. Abner was too old to cope with this. It would fall to her husband to work up some plan to deal with raids in the future. She sighed. More talk. More praying, more requests and bargains with the Lord. More visits from neighbouring headmen who would have to be fed and entertained. Maybe he was right. Maybe prayer would help.

She thought about their eldest child, a daughter as little given to fountains of words as her mother. She was her mother's rock. What she said, she meant, and when she meant something, it came to pass.

She drove the goats among the huts, turning them over to other women, accepting their sympathies for her burned home, her prolix husband. She felt more at peace with herself. Her home had stopped smouldering. Her husband stood by the embers, kicking the charred remains of another marriage bed. The skirt of his tunic held a bundle.

She put her hand on his shoulder, for kindness. She was not given to tenderness. 'What's that?' He opened the bundle; a sooty jumble of loom weights and most of the carved bone shuttle. He closed it again, giving her a tight smile. 'We'll rebuild,' she said. 'With the Lord's help.'

'I've prayed,' he said. 'I've offered Him the sacrifice of whatever comes down that path next. I don't care if it's that brown goat of Abner's. I'll offer it – we'll all offer it – as a burnt offering to God. I mean it. I know you think I'm all talk, but what else have we got? We're babes before warriors. The only arrows I've got are the words I fire up to heaven.' He stared down the road balefully, willing something to appear. 'We are the children of Israel, Adah, and He is the Lord. Our father, not theirs. Not theirs.'

A busy father, she thought, rubbing his back and looking without interest at the road. Maybe something small would come. A coney. A lame goat. That was all He deserved, this neglectful, capricious father who turned to help his children only when they had fallen down and were rolling around in the net. 'I know, Jephthah, I know.'

A shadow appeared on the road ahead of them.

Triphane

Yet not as I will, but as you will.
Gospel of Matthew 26:39

Three times he has had the chance to escape. Or perhaps we should say, three times he has been aware of the cleavages deep within himself and recognized that he can save himself by following one rift. Why can't he do this, eminently sensible and eminently human course? Perhaps because it is so human, and he is not - not quite, though he cannot say whether he is less or more.

The first time was in his childhood. Sitting among the old men and their scrolls, he asked questions about their reading and reacted to what they said with a child's candour. *What's the use of studying all this law*, he said, waving his small grubby hand at the scroll. *If we know it, if we have it in our heads, why do you have to write it down?*

Because it's the Lord's way of talking to us, kid. It's the instructions for making the world the way the Lord wants it.

Like an architect's plan? Like his notes?

The old men fall silent, struck by this. *Yes*, one says slowly, *the law is to the Lord what the plans are to an architect.*

But why, he persists, *would WE need them? Wouldn't they just show us how far from the plan we've gone? How much we've failed?*

But then his father is behind him, sweeping him up off the rug, half-relieved, half-angry, saying *There you are, do you know how worried we've been? We had to come back for you. Everyone else has gone on ahead! Why didn't you tell us?*

Outside, his mother held him very tightly for a long moment, pressing him so hard against her that he could hear the double thrum of her heart and that of the child she carried. Then she pushed him away and looked at him with wan eyes. *Couldn't you have spared a thought for us?*

He saw that he had been moved by something larger than an ignorance of time, or an interest in the old men's eager arguments. Some veil had closed off the rest of the day and for a while caused him to drift along on an unseen current like a seed blown by a strange wind. This wind was some other, fearful part of himself of which he was rarely aware. It felt like the short, premonitory sounds made on the shofar before the greater blast. He himself, he thought, looking at his hands and seeing them with foreign eyes, was and was not this greater thing. He ruthlessly ignored his parents' fears, their love, their small and hard lives, even his own boy's body. As for how this everyday self and the greater, whispering thing, were connected, he could not understand it.

He mumbled something to his mother about business and fathers, made promises he hoped to keep, and ran up the line of travellers, hoping to find friends.

He remembers this conversation, and the fatigue in his mother's eyes ten years later, when he sits on an outcrop looking over the desert, feeling the same fracturing he had felt as a boy. It is many times worse now. He has seen his sisters and sisters-in-law double over, gasping, at the raw shock of bones separating from bones as their skeleton was reorganized around their first child. Perhaps this was what his soul was doing. The second presence he had felt in the temple is there again. Again closing off the world and brushing the sand away from a path which his feet seemed already upon. It is remote, frightening, inflexible, loveless. It whispers that none of this waterless world around him is worth much or for long.

He crouches on the outcrop and longs for something to eat, but he has sworn not to, until hunger has made clear the two voices whispering on either side of the fracture within him. Wild thoughts come and go; stones shimmer and become bread, then stone again. Rock hyraxes skip about like devils. A leopard emerges from a cave and stares in surprise, like a prince waking from his cool sleep to the sight of a beggar, and stalks off.

He wrestles with the other plane of himself. *What do you want from me? What's the point of you – I'm a simple man, meant for a simple life. Leave. You frighten me with myself. I could throw myself off this cliff because I fear what you'll make me do.*

But the voice whispers back *Do it and angels will catch you. There is no escape from me, because I am your very self. I sound different in the same way that your mother sounds different when she talks to herself. What I want; what I planned – you'll do.*

Weeping, despairing, he asks why this plan involves only suffering and a terrible death. He dreads it, even as the shadows fall across the desert like vast wings. *I haven't asked for any of it! I've never asked for anything.*

But in the cool night a voice, sounding like a father such as Joseph has never been, assures him. All the kingdoms of the world, and a death worse than any he could foresee.

Ten more years and the voices have separated entirely. He prays to himself, begs himself not to make himself go through this thing which looms, both absolutely unbearable and absolutely necessary. It is necessary because only its unbearable nature makes it work. Nothing short of the torture and death of his exhausted body, which was once the little boy rolling on the rugs in the temple, stirring wood shavings in the sun, the dark reflection in the leopard's eye - his death alone can save a world he is only half-convinced deserves saving.

Now, in the night air he smells the perfume of an almond tree someone has planted in the olive grove. The third fracture is clear now. It is a striation which connects the two planes of himself, and his soul is a birdlike thing of faith or confidence, flitting between the cold remote force that makes the cracks, and the man who tires and loves and weeps and cannot follow his friends into old age. He slides down a tree and crouches on the ground, his legs shaking, his stomach watery and protesting.

For a brief second, all times and persons collapse into one. There is a wholeness, the planes of self merge and open into a passageway out, out to life, to ordinariness, to anywhere but this night garden of terrors. Just as rapidly, it decoheres and his triphane self reasserts itself. He becomes aware of firelight around him, a hand on his shoulder, lips on his cheek.

Switch

Heaven was opened and he saw the spirit of God descending like a dove and alighting on him.
Gospel of Matthew 3:17

Two men, washing each other clean in a river, duck beneath the ripples. It's not terribly deep. They're in a sort of pool, a little out of the main body of the river, which is brown from the silt of the dry banks. When the men resurface, their identities have become tangled. Their friends, sitting on the dusty riverbank, do not catch this exchange, but it happens nonetheless. Like two girls whose long hair becomes tangled and snarled as it floats and entwines in the bath, the two men emerge feeling as if they have lost something personal and gained something foreign. Like wearing someone else's sandals. Your size, but not your tread.

The two men (who are actually cousins) have always been similar, and the family stories which surround them have been similarly extraordinary. Their mothers have always been quite like each other – it is through their mothers that they are cousins, even though the women and their sons are far apart in age. Their fathers have also been like each other. The cousins and their parents have formed a kind of symmetry, in the way that family groups sometimes do.

Although it is cloudy and too cold for a proper swim, their friends and some more of their family have wandered down to the river through the groves of olive and elder trees and now sit on the banks chatting, pulling and plaiting rushes, wondering how much fish you could get from such muddy water. The cousins are standing together, knee deep in the water, and everyone else is minding their own business. Then they walk a few steps further out and submerge together, the way everyone does when they are kids. It would be no surprise to see two pairs of waving legs emerge as they do a handstand on the bottom.

But they come back up, the water streaming off them, sweeping back wet hair with their hands, rubbing it out of their beards. They wade back to the bank, clutch each other's arms, and start wringing the water out of their shirts, their thin loincloths.

Maybe the sun breaks through the clouds. Maybe it even seems to tear them open.

So much hangs on a moment. Unseen perhaps even by heaven, two cousins sneakily exchange identities beneath the muddy river so that they can both get what they crave. They are already so close, what does it matter, who does which action? It's all the same family.

Things merge into things. The question of who sees the incredible thing is forgotten. What they saw, or claimed to see it – that's important. The frames that separate one cousin's experience from everyone else's blur. In the future, the cousins will get muddled up, and what really happened will be lost in a veil of words.

So much hangs on one word: εἶδεν. He saw.

The younger cousin leaves with his friends. They show him the solicitude that friends reserve for the one who is a little strange, prone to fantasising, or perhaps a bit weak-minded. As they're all ambling along, straggling on the road, he suddenly says that when he was in the river he saw the clouds part, violently, and the breath of God – the friends look at each other a bit sadly, because this is evidently one of his bad days – the breath of God come out of the sky like a pretty dove.

A dove? they say patiently.

Yes, yes, he says. He makes fluttering motions with his hands. *Soft, grey, plump-breasted. So gentle. It just settled on me. Like a puff of air. Like a kiss.*

Doves aren't river birds, one of them says with a snort. He gets an elbow in the ribs and someone says, *Don't be an arsehole, Thomas.*

But the cousin isn't bothered. *I said* like *a dove. But not...*

52

And what else? says someone, trying to be kind.

A voice.

Oh yeah? Where from? Whose voice?

From heaven. It said, 'You are my son, beloved, and I am truly pleased in you.'

The kind one gives him a gentle punch on the arm. *Yeah mate, he should be. You're a good bloke.*

Better not tell your dad that, Thomas says. *He might feel a bit put out if you say your dad's in heaven.*

How come I never see these things? Or no one in heaven says they're well pleased with me? another one moans.

Yeah, I wonder, says someone. There is a gentle ripple of laughter.

The cousin looks back and sees John, his cousin, his other self, still standing by the river, looking at the sunlight dancing on the ripples. Then he turns away and keeps walking down the road in the direction of the highway with his friends.

Which man saw these things? Later, much later, when all the stories are put together end to end, little discrepancies will become clear. One version will say that the younger cousin saw the heavens open, the spirit descend, and the voice speak to him. Another version will say that the voice spoke to others about him. A third will not bother to mention that only the cousin saw these things. A fourth will say that it was the older cousin who saw and heard them. By the time the discrepancies are evident and problematic, so many terrible things will have been done in the name of this story that an accumulated guilt and filth will have filled the cracks between versions. Flushing it all out would crack the story like an old plate.

Whatever these two, inextricably tangled, men saw and heard beneath the water, it seems that no one else witnessed it on that grey day. Two cousins from a family marked by madness and suffering ducked out of sight for a moment, and tried to evade, scrub off, or exchange those hallucinations which they fear – and hope - will no longer torment only themselves.

The Best and Worst of Gods

… when the Æsir would not loose Fenrir, then he bit off the hand at the place now called 'the wolf's joint;' and Týr is one-handed, and is not called a reconciler of men.

Gylfaginning

They're not my gods, you say. Perhaps. But every seventh day you recall Tiw, the best and worst of the gods.

Thor looked narrowly at Tiw, the dark god who stood always off to one side, observing proceedings, making sure that oaths were kept and battle conducted fairly. The god of thunder frequently disagreed with Odin Allfather, but they agreed about Tiw – he annoyed them both senseless.

'Where did he even come from?' Thor asked Heimdall. Guardian of the Bifrost, the colour-glittering road between worlds, Heimdall saw every coming and going – except Tiw's. Heimdall shrugged, his golden eyes never leaving the many worlds on Yggdrasil. 'Tiw was here before us, before Asgard and Valhalla, before the Bifrost. He came on a wave of words from the east, where they call him Deywos.'

But Thor was already gone. Gods do not like to be reminded that even they come from somewhere. 'What do we need him for?' he said to the Allfather, who had given up an eye in return for wisdom. 'He's unlike us, and his insistence on oaths sticks in my craw.' Thor banged Mjöllnir, the hammer forged for his hand alone; somewhere on the World Ash, kingdoms fell and millions perished.

'We need him precisely because he's unlike us,' said Odin distantly. 'He has been here from the beginning, and he will have a hand in holding back the end.' Then he fell silent, which meant that even Odin did not fully understand the knowledge he possessed. He was simply bound, by the pain he had endured as he hung on the tree for nine days and nights, to recount what he knew.

Thor left in disgust. But he was afraid, too, because the High One had alluded to the terrible time: Ragnarök. The end of all things, which every living thing feels drawn towards, and which makes even the gods despair.

Ragnarök, Odin knew somehow – though he could not have said how and wished he did not know – would come about when the monstrous children of Loki, the Trickster, the Liar, Inverter of the Right Order, Lord of the Prank Pushed Too Far, Patron of the Broken Promise, God of the Friend-Turned-Cruel, when his children brought an end to this pretty world and everything in it. Such monsters come into being because the gods do not obey their own rules. That it would be Tiw who suffered the very first wound of Ragnarok, aeons before it came about, seemed both right and dreadful to Grimnir, the Hooded One.

And it would go like this.

The bringer of the end will be the giant wolf Fenrir. Born of Loki and a Jötunn, Fenriswolf has a mouth as big as the sky. When he opens his jaws, his top teeth form the vault of the heavens, and his tongue will lap up the ocean where lives his sister, the Jörmungandr. But even Fenrir was a baby once. A wolf puppy, soft and trusting, liquid-eyed and little. Because they cannot yet kill one another the Æsir allow Fenrir to live, but in misery. Unloved, unfed, unhoused, the Fenriscub can only turn wicked.

In the Fimbulvetr, men will say, 'If only the gods had shown some love to Fenrir – even once.' And as the world is consumed by cold, we will remember that it is not lack of riches, or skill, or justice that you die from, but lack of love.

So there was Fenrir, great and unloved, roaming the fields around Asgard. The gods knew he had to be fed, but not one had the courage to do it. Only Tiw took meat and threw it to the wolf, because it was the right and the brave thing to do and because he was so old that he could remember when gods were both good and brave.

Fenriswolf fed, and looked at Tiw with his great golden eyes, and was a little grateful. And Tiw looked at Fenrir and foresaw in the neglect of the wolf all our ends.

The wolf grew, the gods feared, and they conspired to bind him. They had the dwarves make Gleipnir. This was a fetter constructed of impossible things – a woman's beard, a mountain's roots, a cat's footfall, a bird's spit, a fish's breath, a bear's sinews. Thus is the wolf – the truest thing in Asgard, clear as ice, simpler than the sun – hobbled by ignoble things, words and the snares of thought.

They brought Gleipnir to the island Lyngvi where Fenrir lived, alone and hated, torn from his mother and family, reviled amid the green leaves and the other creatures. Fenrir looked at the gods, boozy with mead and their own power, and despaired. Thor the bully, Odin the deceiver, smiling Frey and Freya who appear only when the hard work is done – Fenrir despised them all, and himself too for longing for a soft touch from even one of their hands.

'What would you, Allfather?' Fenrir said, although the name *father* curdled in his throat. 'Another test of my strength?'

'You broke the last two chains easily,' said Odin. 'You are called Hròðvitnir, the Fame Wolf. Live up to your name by testing yourself on a third.' He brought out Gleipnir, and Fenrir felt the dwarves' magic radiating from the pretty thing, which was thin as a ribbon of silk and intractable as impossible things always are. And Fenrir looked at Tiw, who blushed at the deception, and every head on the island held the same thought: *This is a trick; the gods are without honour; and yet it must be done.*

'I will not bind myself with it,' said Fenrir sadly, 'because you and I both know that I will never be free.' He could feel the jaws of fate closing around him, but still, even the battle-wolf of the splendid sky-shield did not want to submit so meekly, or let his captors go unbloodied. He had to have something to comfort him in the long aeons during which he will lie, feared, bound, and waiting for the end.

'We will give you a bond,' said Odin, the Bale-Worker, the Riddler, the Blind Guest, 'a pledge that we will remove the fetter if you cannot get free.' His promise fell like a stone, as the gods' promises always do.

'Let one of you put his hand in my mouth,' said Fenrir, 'while I test this fetter. If I am not freed, the hand will be lost, and will remind men for all time that you cannot trust a god.'

They winced at this and each one looked at the other, hoping someone else would volunteer to put their hand in the mouth of Fenriswolf.

Why did Tiw step forward? Did he do it as the lord of oaths-after-battle? The patron of the Thing where men hammer out disputes? Or because he alone had fed Fenrir from a puppy, lost and howling for his mother, loved by none, whose little misery is evidence of how unworthy the gods really are? We cannot tell: we know only what the gods do, rarely why.

But Tiw put his hand between Fenrir's jaws as the fetter was wound around the wolf's legs. They looked at each other in sorrow and profound understanding that by this action, they both lost: Tiw lost his honour, and Fenrir his freedom. Then Fenrir strained against Gleipnir, which tightened even as he pulled, and he knew it would never come off until everything, *everything* – the sun, the moon, the sound of a cat's step, even sound itself – is ending. He struggled all the long heavenly day against the fetter, and he would never ask the gods to release him.

They stood and laughed uneasily, then more heartily when Fenrir closed his jaws and took the hand that had fed him, and Tiw shouted in both pain and shame. The Aesir departed, leaving the wolf bound, and the god who had been the best, now the worst, destroyed. And Tiw and Fenrir lay on Lyngvi and knew that they had become bywords. We remember them every seven days; we will remember them when we hear the wolf at the door, when we see any man and mistreated creature who will eventually be the death of each other.

Ragnarök

Winter shall last three years. No crops shall grow, nor shall there be fodder for the beasts. The weak shall die of cold and hunger.

All over the world shall be strife and suffering. Brother shall kill brother for what little food and fuel remains.

Managarmr shall feed upon the slain, grow strong and devour Mani, splashing blood on the benches of Valhalla, signaling the beginning of the Great Battle. His brother, Sköll, shall devour the sun. There shall be a great earthquake and Fenrir shall be released for the final battle.

The Prophecy of Mimir

I was going up the south stair in the Bodleian, passing a window, when I looked out and saw snow falling in the courtyard, and it occurred to me that Fenrir was an object of great pity.

I must have been near the end of my time at Oxford, because I remember the feeling of that moment: always winter and never Christmas. It was typical of how I thought at that time, to be going up for a book about who knew what, and suddenly to realize that my thoughts were somewhere entirely different, occupied with the end of things, of being savaged, of cold and pity.

I have always preferred the story of Ragnarök to the Christian apocalypse, which rings no bells for those of us who grew up cold. Apocalypse is full of abstruse terms that only make sense in Greek. It holds out a false promise of a singular, definitive ending with a lot of noise and judgment and fire. Ragnarök is closer to the experience of a Scottish childhood: an endless deepening freeze which kills you by making you shiver yourself to bits. You die exhausted, in agony from shaking, all your joints pulling apart from each other, forcing you, creaking, to your knees while you're still alive. The Apocalypse, by contrast, just makes you realize you were wrong.

Ragnarök shows you that you are weak. It has the lordly disregard for your individual actions, the quavery goodness of your tissue-paper soul, that only a natural force (or possibly Oxford) can have. Ragnarök says, *Nobody cares.*

I would never see the Winter of Swords. Oxford had made it abundantly clear that I would die in the Fimbulvetr. I couldn't even withstand the deep freeze of English academics and their catamite graduate students. I couldn't see my way through the battlefield of Wednesday seminars in the History of the Book Room, where a handful of them sat, hunched like vultures over the carrion of their careers. It was a weekly two-hour torture to watch them stripping the carcasses of nascent careers they'd derailed or simply cut off from human warmth and sincerity until they withered and died.

But still, I felt for Fenrir, whom the Norse made the manifestation of that drive to feed on others. Wolves are not really like that. Wolves are everything we are not: devoted, loyal, frugal, humourous, unpitying of themselves. This was why I pitied the figure I thought was Fenrir in the Bodleian courtyard's drifting snow and freezing English dark, and wondered which of us was more of a prisoner.

Dam

Heo under heolfre genam
cupe folme.
Beowulf

Here is a story: wave-wind. Shining rock. The reflection of yourself in a seal's eye. Water crash, slip and drain, sudden spume, and the small still world of a tidepool. Lie on the grey flint edges as the sea smashes up and around you; spindrift spits and settles and soothes you, who are too vast to be taken by the silver spread's suck and draw.

You sit on the sea stacks and the world's weather is your moods. There is no difference between you and the all-around. Look! The clouds appear twice – in the sky and the sea. Between them, you are a finger scoured by twin water-worlds. They fight over you like two sisters over a baby.

You are all this, the welkin and the wave, bog, forest, shadow, screech of eating, eaten, full, sleep.

Then a stranger comes, like you but bigger, sour-smelling. There are dreams of teeth, gripping, pain and warmth with another. Then the long sleep of winter when the gripping one goes, taking his scent with him.

You wake, fatter and full of a new world. Now you have weather within. Your own whale road rocks, the Bifrost between your legs pours forth, down which a shining crying thing slides. You have spent months looking within. Now you look up and around – the world has shut its mouth to you. You are no longer part of the rustle, the goings-on beneath Ymir's Skull.

The shining child girns and clings, bites, sucks and draws. He is your own tide-bringer. He draws out of your bone-cavern the heart's whole hoard. Fettered by this squealer, you are now separate from the world, which is so many dangers to him. You were in the world as wind was: godless, mindless, unfearful. Now you have new gods, and they are fearful: Hunger, Cold, Tears in the Dark, the Fall from Heights, Struggle in the Sea, the Tree-Burners, Ring-Wearers, the Killing Ones. And your little weapons are Lullaby, Breast, Kiss, and Fish.

Now he is grown and the world reaches its long arms to take you back, with wind-lick, wave-spit, rock-warmth again. You cannot go. Fear-fettered, you are trapped in the cave which is home, by the thought of the shining child who is now a man, your light-jewel, the cinder of heaven which fell from your guts, your storm, your summer, your fire. When he comes back, gore-maddened and blood-glutted, you know that if you lost him, the whole world would be only pain and noise.

Linden

...*schône sanc diu nahtegal.*
Walter von der Vogelweide

The tank's original driver, Tom, had died at Bayreuth. Not heroically; a dog had bitten him, the bite had gone bad, and he had died of sepsis within 72 hours.

Now, rumbling into Zwettl, Bayle had almost mastered steering. In theory it was easy; the two levers controlled the tracks, and you could go forward or backwards. Throwing the levers in opposite directions gave you a sharp turn. He had been the loader before Tom died. All he had had to do was load the shells, flip the hatch, and toggle the switch to lock it. Now Sanchin was the commander, Zip the new loader and Nizeti the gunner. Sanchin performed double duty as Bayle's guide, yelling directions from his hatch. It was agreed that Bayle wasn't capable of any position other than driving because he locked up under stress, as the vast and vicious consequences of his actions paralysed him. He had flat feet and a hyper-sprung moral compass.

Looking through the driver's scope, he saw the main square of Zwettl. The fountains still played and a huge rococco monument stood before the konditorein and gasthäuser. The tank ahead of him in the convoy released a sharp machine-gun cough and the hand was blown off a beautiful rococco youth, who stood gesturing with his stump to the spring sky. Bayle swallowed and twitched the levers, trying to skirt around the rubble. He imagined the stone hand lying on the cobbles and wondered if it could be repaired.

Thinking about the hand, he drifted a few degrees away from the tank ahead. Through the smeary scope he saw a linden tree like a light green girl on the edge of the Dreifaltigkeits Platz, twirling her dress of leaves. He shuddered forward. He remembered a poem about a linden

62

tree. Some medieval thing learned years ago, when he still went to classes and still heard music that wasn't Big Band or dixie. He tried to send his mind above the tank racket and Sanchin's continual yelling. What was the poem?

Under der linden, an der heide something something something...

He realized he was slewing towards the tree. He hauled on the levers, remembered to downshift, got his hands and feet mixed up, and brought Hank to a heavy stop just shy of the sapling. Sanchin released a string of profanities from the cupola. Zip leaned forward and rested his head on the gunner's scope, which he did whenever Bayle's higher thought processes got in the way of the war.

Bayle's hands were trembling on the levers. *Tandaradei*, he whispered, feeling foolish and weak with gladness. Whatever other terrible things he had to do, he had spared the little linden tree.

'Can we fucking go now?' said Sanchin, ducking down from his perch. 'You're holding up a fucking division, you faggoty airy-fairy fuck.'

'I don't...how do I...,' Bayle wiped his hands down his shirt and mashed the gears again. If he lurched forward he would crush the tree. He didn't know how to get Hank going in reverse. He was still struggling with the song in the back of his memory.

'Get the fuck going!' Sanchin yelled, popping out of the split hatch. 'Go! Go fucking forward! You can't go back – you've got Dilley up your ass!'

Bayle stared at the levers. It came to him. Walter von der Vogelweide, the minnesinger. A love song about a couple under a linden tree. He felt sick.

Sanchin popped down again and grabbed Bayle by the back of his shirt like a recalcitrant puppy. 'Do I have to do everything my fucking self?'

Bayle shook his head. He was weeping openly. Zip and Nizeti looked at the oil gauges, embarrassed. A green leaf fell before the scope.

Bayle threw the levers and they lurched forward.

Under der linden
an der heide,
dâ unser zweier bette was,
dâ muget ir vinden
schône beide
gebrochen bluomen unde gras.
vor dem walde in einem tal,
tandaradei,
schône sanc diu nahtegal.

Herodis

And as son as he to me cam,
Wold ich, nold ich, he me nam,
And made me with him ride
Opon a palfray bi his side
King Orfeo

Herodis stands in the doorway of the beggar's house and watches her husband as he heads towards the castle. He has slung his harp, wrapped in a cloth, over one shoulder; with his long beard and grey head he looks like every other minstrel in every other fairytale. But he walks like the king he was, she thinks, and will be again, when his steward returns the kingdom to him after ten long years.

Herodis turns away into the gloomy little house.

They have been there for three nights, since Orfeo rescued her from the Faery King's dreadful fortress where she had dreamed for a decade. Why did they not go straight to the castle? Why did they not head from the cleft in the rock to the castle gate, rejoicing, demanding the instant return of the throne, crown, and kingdom which Orfeo relinquished when he set off on his ten-year search for her?

Because she had not bled, she thinks. He had to be sure that she was not carrying a half-breed, a faery's child, born from that terrible mistake under the fair impe-tree so long ago.

That morning she bled. He picked up his harp and set off for the castle, happy.

It is over for him, Herodis knows. Orfeo has won. He has his homecoming. He can be happy. But Herodis, standing in the gloom of the beggar's house, knows that it can never be over. The grim, pale figure of the Faery King, and the lead weight of his inexorable power, will stand always just behind her, just a little out of sight. She can never be entirely safe. Nor, she suspects, can she ever be entirely happy.

65

But how did she stray into the Faery King's shadow, like spindrift around a sail?

It was May. A hot morning in the orchard, white and yellow flowers between the trees and her husband playing the harp beneath a medlar tree in full bloom. Birds calling one to the other from the green boughs. And Herodis – she was barefoot, the grass still cool and wet beneath her soles. And her women…ah yes, the sweep of skirts and, yes, tresses flying as they danced a ring around a pear tree. And then spinning and spinning down and down until she lay between her ladies, her hair spread on their silk skirts. And she looked up among the green branches and closed her eyes in bliss beneath a fair impe-tree.

And slept.

The ladies watched her, pretty Herodis, Orfeo's queen, and looked at each other full of unease. Who would dare wake her? To sleep under any tree is to give yourself up to the world. To sleep under an impe-tree, a grafted thing bearing the slips of different fruit, is to leave yourself open to the Other world, which has its own order and abhors the things man makes.

Back and forth raced Herodis' eyes beneath her fair eyelids as she dreamed something wild and dreadful. They held her head tightly between their white hands, but they would not wake her. Not only because it is a queen's privilege to sleep where and when she will, but because we make our choices and we bear what comes of them – or we don't. This is known as life.

The sun arced across the sky, the undertide was gone, noon came and went and the thing was done. Then Herodis woke with a blood-curdling scream, and the storm broke upon the realm of Orfeo, the harper-king.

It took six men to hold Herodis' hands, to bind her with her own girdle and carry her bodily to bed, where she screamed and wept. The blood from her scratches ran down her face and her gown, so lately full of orchard blossoms, was rent with long tears of desperation. Orfeo knelt by her bed and twined his long fingers around hers and begged her to say what ailed her.

Pretty Herodis turned her face to the wall and said, 'I have loved you as much as I have loved my own life, and now—' and she cried as if her heart had broken. Orfeo crawled up onto the bed and wrapped himself around her closer than the lappet around his harp. 'And what?' he said. 'And now what?'

'And now I must leave you.'

And Orfeo, whose life until then had been the life of a man in a pleasant dream or a fairytale, felt the icy fingers of something called the World, and was aghast.

'Sleeping under the impe-tree, I felt the ground shake with the approach of many riders, and I stood because suddenly they were upon me, the troop of the Other King. Ten fair men, armed as captains and pale as death. They drew rein before me, in our very orchard – as if we had no walls, and I no lord.

' "Come with us," they said, "right quick, madam. Our king, whom you know, wishes your company."

'I caught the bridle of the leader, and it burned like ice in my hand. "I know of no king except my own marriage lord, and those in the realms over the seas – and your lord is surely none of those."

'The leader turned his pale eyes upon me and said, "You know the Other King, as everyone in this waking world does. You have always known him. He is the darkness that breathes by your bed at night. He is the trembling at the prospect of pain, the arms into which the battle-dead fall. He is the fear in your heart when you break a sworn oath; he is the pale power which balances this life."

'Oh my love! You know him, and I do too. And I told that Pale King's captain that I would not, could not, go with him. They wheeled about and left me a little, only to return faster than an ember flickers. The ground shook again, and through this green place of tender trees came that Other King, with all his court. A hundred silent men and ladies on white horses, beautiful and empty as drained wineskins. And among them he, whom we have always known, whose gaze is as close as the heart in your chest.

'My will was not my own. He made me ride with him on a palfrey at his side. I had no thoughts as I went because he had me enspancelled and I belonged to him for that little space, as all the company did. He rode me through that Other place where it is always high summer, and brought me back to the impe-tree where I saw myself asleep as a bird caught in glass.

' "Look upon yourself, madam," he said. "And return tomorrow beneath the slip-tree where you sleep now. You will go with us and live forever in the summer realm. And if you make us fetch you, it will be the worse for you. Better never born than torn apart as you'll be."

'And I woke and saw the sky above the impe-tree. I have given myself up for lost, my dove, and so must you.'

Orfeo heard all this without listening because he was a man and a king. The castle was up all night. The night went like a slave and the dawn came like a work-day. Mid-morning was damp and grey and everyone was apt to take the whole thing as a joke. But Herodis lay in bed, gray and shattered as seawrack. Still, a hundred knights in armour attended Herodis to the orchard, joking and privately thinking Orfeo was mad. They made a shiltron around Herodis, looked with menace into the noontime drizzle and wondered if perhaps they would all be bored to death.

Noon came and went and she was twitched away amid them, silently as rain.

Of the tumult that followed, we shall pass over.

Orfeo was carried to the bed which still stank of Herodis' tears. He lay there, bereft of breath by the might of how things turn out. The eye of this story will fly up, lark-like, high enough to gaze over a ten-year space. In that time, Orfeo will give up his kingdom, appoint his steward in his place, and take to the woods with his harp. He will wrap his sword in rags and hide it in a hollow tree, take on the wildness of that forest and give himself up to a despair that the throne forbids. It is a long and private liturgy, a wordless arbor into which we cannot see, now sere, now blooming, now wan.

Orfeo became an old man. When the weather was clear he took up his harp and played to the wild things, but his music frightened them. On some hot noon days the Other King came with his rout, blowing and crying, the hounds baying and thrashing their tails, taking no quarry and scenting only Orfeo's blood. He saw the Pale King with banners flying, attended by a thousand fine silent riders. The King looked down at him from his pale horse with an austere, hollow-eyed smile. At other times they came to his clearing to dance with tabours and trumpets that Orfeo could not hear. Then they broke and vanished, leaving him struggling with the wrapping of a rusted blade, weeping the hoarse, hot tears of an old man.

One day the Faery King came riding with an escort sixty ladies' strong, no other man among them. Each woman bore on her hand a falcon in token of the trapped bird the Pale King had made of her, and they rode, unseeing and unsmiling, by the river to hunt waterfowl, releasing the birds when the Pale King bid them, looking into a grey sky as their falcons slew and slew and slew. From the other bank of the grey river Orfeo met the King's eye, and they gazed at each other through a dreadful blizzard of blood and feathers. The Other King gave Orfeo a small smile and turned his mount to go, calling to him a fair rider whom Orfeo recognized as his own once-queen.

Orfeo shouted to Herodis, who turned in her saddle and stared silently across the river that none may cross without the Pale King's nod, and not a word could she speak. Tears spilled down her face; the other women drew in close to her and made her ride away with them. Shouting, Orfeo ran alongside the river and watched until they came to a hill and passed through into it, going to that Other place.

And so Orfeo, thin and grey as a winter twig, seamed with dirt and sorrow, clad in rags and carrying his harp, went through the rock to the Other place where Herodis was. Three miles of summer country led him to a hundred-towered castle which had never known an enemy and never would. To the gate Orfeo went, as a man in a dream, and shouted for the porter.

'What would you, sir?'

Play for the lord of the place, Orfeo said. *For solace and joy, if he needs one and can feel the other.* The porter's lips twitched at the joke, and he let Orfeo in. Past the gate house, and into the inner ward went Orfeo, clutching his harp and trying not to notice the rich garden of suffering. Lying by the walls, some were dead and some on the brink of death. Some had no head, some no arms, some were battle-dead and others had been strangled as they sat at table. Some were mad, some drowned, others wizened with fire, some lay dead or insane on their child-beds. Some were curled asleep as they had been in noon-times of the waking world, for there, too, was Herodis, asleep under the ghost of an impe-tree.

Into the silent hall went Orfeo, unopposed. Beneath a shining canopy sat that cruel king and his beautiful queen, a fair woman with a smile like sleet. Pity the dead and the sleepers who are their courtiers.

What do they do all day? wondered Orfeo, even as his heart thrums like a dropped gittern. *What moves them to ride out? How does this king command his troop, this queen her women?* He realized that he had only ever played at ruling, compared to this king's hold over his subjects.

He knelt before the dais. 'O lord,' he said, feeling as if he was speaking in a dream, 'hear my minstrelsy. I have come from far away to play for you.'

The Pale King turned a gelid gaze on the kneeling ragamuffin. 'What are you, that you have come here? I have not sent for you. None of mine have sent for you.' There was a silence. 'No one has come here without my bidding – not since the beginning of the world.'

'Lord, poverty knows neither time nor bidding; it too has obtained since the beginning of the world. My poverty has as illustrious a heritage as your reign and by that right I ask leave to play for you.'

Silenced, the royal pair watched him sit on a small stool, cross his ankles, and pluck a note potent and lasting as honey. Orfeo sang about a realm where seasons run and arc, people age and die, and are forced to choose what they believe. The song of this ragged harper who had wandered in from the world unasked occupied them so much that the Pale Queen's face softened and her husband inclined his head, and neither noticed the crippled creatures who composed their court come creeping in and lie around the singer like dogs who long for a soft touch.

On and on Orfeo sang, wrapping them all in a rich smooth skein of song until the Other King's brow was unlined and his pale hands unclenched. Orfeo stopped at last and the Pale King said, 'It is well, singer. Ask your reward and it will be yours.'

And Orfeo gestured to the sleep-walking figure of Herodis, brought to the hall by his song like the others. 'Sir, give me this lady. I ask nothing else but the fair one who slept under the impe-tree.'

The air cracked. 'I think not,' said the Pale King. 'A sorry couple you would be – a harping beggar and a flawless thing like her.'

'Ah sir,' Orfeo said, his heart shivering in his chest, 'it would be fouler to hear a lie from your mouth, an oath as mangled as are some of these, your courtiers. No, you said just now that what I would have, you would give. And you must keep your word.'

Remote as starlight, the king made a small movement of his hand and Herodis stirred. She rose like a puppet on strings, head-hung and loose-fingered. 'Take her and go,' the king said. 'And do not presume to trespass again. Not everything can be bought with a song.'

His harp under one arm and Herodis' limp hand under the other, Orfeo led her, tripping and shambling like an old woman, from the hall. They were at the door before she turned and looked back at the dais, caught between the two kings who ruled her, and Orfeo pulled her back to the waking world.

Now in the doorway of a beggar's house, Herodis waits for her husband to take back his kingdom in a peal of bells. *You wait to be wooed, to be married,* she thinks. *You wait for children, you wait for the conviction that this is a good life. If it does not come, you wait for the shadow of something else to take you. Then you wait to be saved. In between times, what do you do? Pray. Sing. Sew. Sleep.*

This is not just the lot of women – there are enough bewitched knights and lords at the faery king's castle to show that men too can put themselves in the way of unhappiness and become trapped there.

If you are saved, you spend your life holding your breath, counting your blessings. You have made the world show its hand, and it has marked you so heavily that you can only spend the rest of your life dazed and afraid. The Pale King returns you but he is always there. That's the nature of shadows. You have been someone else's quest; winning you back has been their happiness. Now you must journey out to find yours.

From the castle, a peal of bells rings.

Bisclavret

Ne savez mie que ceo munte.
Mult durement en a grant hunte.
Marie de France, *Lai de Bisclavret*

Inside the wolf, the man sleeps. No wild thing can be blamed for its bloodlust, any more than a woman for her curiosity.

They are everywhere and have many names. Bisclavret, Garwal, Werewolf, Úlfhéðinn. Baptism cannot prevent the change, and no one knows why it comes over some men and not others. We must all bear our trials, and the wolf-man is no different. We act on ungovernable desires – it's simply nature. Without these drives, there would be no stories.

*

She has dimmed since he brought her from her father's house. He tries to make light of it.

'I thought you'd be glad of time to yourself.'

She shakes her head and looks down. She is very young, he remembers. Probably too young to value a few nights alone each week. 'I just want…' More headshaking.

'What?'

'I don't want you to be angry with me. I hate being shouted at.'

'I won't be angry. Why would I shout at you?' He takes her wrist, pulls her towards him as they sit awkwardly on the marriage-bed he is hardly ever in. 'Come on, tell me. What do you want?'

'I just…I want to know where you go every week.' She sees exasperation cross his face. 'It's three nights – every week. I mean, what are you doing? Don't you get hungry? Or cold?' She looks him dead in his hazel eyes. 'I would not believe something as low as another woman. Because you're noble in birth and mind and I know you're better than that.'

She's clever, he thinks, watching her earnest face, so young it can only elicit fondness, admiration, laughter. Clever to put it that way. Shame she's a woman. She'd have been a good cardinal.

'You come home smelling strange,' she says in a low voice, watching him, watching her back. 'Meat and leaf mould and wild places. Do you … are nights in the forest better than my bed?'

'No,' he says quickly. 'It's not that. It has nothing to do with you at all. It's an old … affliction. I've had it all my life and it's just easier to be away when it comes on me.'

She looks openly skeptical. He is handsome, strong, healthy. He hears mass without sorrow, takes the host without pain. And he does not carry himself as one who ails – that hopeless, sad way which makes invalids irritable, exhausted.

They go on like this, her inching into the dark territory of his private life, him giving ground because she will not, could not possibly guess the truth at the heart of it. When it comes out it is like a sudden threat in chess, surprising them both.

'Fine,' he says, and the words are out before he knows what has happened, as if his lips, his voice belong to someone else. 'Fine. I become bisclavret. I go into the forest. I live on small prey – *small* prey,' he says, taking her hand, 'and roots, and river water. I hide deep in the thickest stretches, until it has passed and I can come back. You say it's three nights but wolves know nothing of time, just need and sleep.'

She doesn't snatch her hand back, although they both become conscious of the edges of his touch. The feeling of each other's skin has ceased to mean anything. He is too busy feeling the blood beating in this dense moment to wonder what her next question will be, but it's so surprising that he laughs.

'So are you naked then?'

'What do you mean? Wolves don't wear clothes.'

'Yes, but… I mean, when you change, what becomes of your clothes?'

In retrospect, he sees that he should have paused here. Why would she ask if she didn't know the secrets of the bisclavret? To tell her is to hand over half his power. But what can guilt and duty not push us to do? She is young; they have been married less than a year; she was wooed by many others – and, for all he knows, preferred every one of them to him. Here she is, alone with him in their chamber grappling to understand how she will live out this fantastic problem in the months and years ahead. He owes her an answer.

'I leave my clothes in… a secret place.' He senses her waiting. 'If anyone sees me change, or takes my clothes, I cannot change back.'

Half his power gone. She is still waiting. Now he feels like a rabbit in the wood, with a hunter waiting for him to break cover. When did she learn to be so stealthy?

'How can one who loves you, harm you?' she says softly. Later he will wonder whether this question was academic. Did she love him then? Did she ever love him? Sometimes we put our hand in the fire because we have watched the flame for too long and can imagine nothing else.

'There is a bush near the old chapel, a bow-shot from the woods' far western edge. There I change.' There, he thinks, I am undone. All his power is now hers. They go to bed, but she can no longer lie at his side and turns this way and that, thinking how best she can get herself from him.

She gets out of bed and banks up the fire, spending the rest of the night sewing, stabbing some linen with a needle until she falls asleep in her chair and is woken by the dogs at dawn, whining and licking her feet.

The next night, he is gone. She lies in bed alone, cuddling a cold anger to her. She has realized a more pressing fact: any child begotten by him may share his affliction. How do you carry a wolf's child? How do you bear it without discovery? She trembles when she remembers that his mother did not survive his birth.

She writes to a neighbour, one who had wooed her before her marriage. He has not ceased to pursue her – politely, of course. Tastefully, but persistently. *What you hope for is yours*, she writes, *if you will come and do me a single service before three days are over.*

He's there within the hour.

Cagey, with the faith in oaths that you only see in oath-breakers, she swears her lover to secrecy. Thus, by the kiss of his wife is the bisclavret betrayed. The dogs sit unhappily at her feet. They want to be out in the night forest, where the woman's lover and her husband are hunting each other among the black trunks, the shadows of things that lurk and prowl and are private and best left alone.

Her lover returns; her husband does not.

In a chest in the chamber where she now sleeps alone and easily, is a suit of clothes, slowly losing the heat and scent of the man who once wore them.

How easily we accept astonishing things! One cold afternoon the lord's mesnie and peasants turn out and beat the withered grass until sundown, looking for his body – or parts of it. Nothing is found, and although his wife is pale and sighing, they admit defeat and drink deeply of the hot ale the lady has generously provided for the search. The lord's people agree that the forest has taken him. He was a good lord and can be honestly mourned – and everyone should stay close to the keep and under each other's eye.

The king is informed of his friend's disappearance which, it is suggested, is due to some ferocious forest beast who has left the lady a widow. He sorrows for his friend and tries not to count the number of friends he has lost to treachery, mishap, war, disease, marriage, and holy orders. Such transformations are the will of God, he thinks. He is a king and must bear his loneliness.

Then one day, long after the lord's disappearance, after the lady's marriage to the neighbour who had wooed her so hard, the king rides into their lands with his hunt. The wolf, asleep in his den, wakes in a drench of fear. The hounds' scent darkens the sky like a shower of arrows. He is up and out of the den and running through shade, through stream, over the spoor of other heart-sick chased things, through cleft, over cliff, until he can no more and feels his half-man's soul running beyond his legs, and he drops, his flanks heaving under a merciless sky.

They are all around him – the dogs, the horses, the runners and dog boys, and last into the clearing, the king. With the last of his breath, the wolf slinks to that well-known foot, richly booted and silver-spurred, and puts a futile paw on the shining stirrup. There is a general cry, at once for the king's safety and surprise at the beast's apparent wit.

'Hold.' Does the royal eye look into that far nobler eye, golden among the green leaves in this spring world of death which man brings to everything? Does he see his friend? Or does the intelligent part of the king cleave to the same part in the wolf, and revile the idea of harming that which approaches him?

'Rein in the dogs.' The hounds, confused and disappointed, are called off. The racket in the wolf's head, of fear and noise which men always bring, abates. 'Let's go. Leave him. This is not…not what I hunt.' The king casts a last, considering look into those deep golden eyes and wheels his courser around. There are noises of dismay, protests. 'The dogs'll be set back, sir, to find the quarry and have none of it. They're like peasants – they only understand work if there's blood at the end of it.' There is laughter, from the mounted men. Not from the runners.

'Sir, we've ridden hard toda–'

'I will hunt no more, my lord of Orleans, and neither will you, unless you find a blind rabbit on our way back.'

But as he kicks the courser homewards, the wolf lunges desperately after him, keeping pace alongside the king like an aestel leading the eye along the page to the meaning of it all. Astonished, charmed, something within the king flares hopefully and he calls off the servants who would chase the wolf away.

On through the forest, to the verges, the villages, and the keep, the wolf and riders go, sticking to the royal figure like birdlime – but only the wolf is allowed to follow him to his chamber, to lie on the sheepskins by the bed and, in the night, clamber up to the sleeping man and cover him, twitching and unhappy in his royal dreams, with the heaviness of wolf sleep.

The truth is that, within days, the wolf is loved by the king with the love that only animals can draw from our imperfect hearts. A lonely man, exhausted by the vagaries and viciousness of other, human, desires, the king finds that he can at last sink into love like sleep. What a relief, he finds, to whisper *I love you* to the great wise head, and feel its golden gaze on him without calculation or heat.

The court knows that the wolf must not be harmed – this is not hard, because he is loveable, quiet, tactful, affectionate, and has the king's ear. Not a few knights are told to look at the wolf as a mirror of knightly behaviour. He harms no one and bears himself like a maiden: chaste, humble, gracious.

Until, that is, the wife who betrayed him comes to court, bringing her new husband. The scent of his betrayers is hardly in the air of the great hall before the wolf has flown snarling at them, before an aghast crowd.

And bitten her nose off.

There is blood. Screaming. The king, brandishing a stick, raining blows that the wolf does not feel. Finally, the wolf is hauled off and locked up in disgrace.

Watching it all is the king's most privy counsellor, a man who loves a mystery even more than he loves his lord. Why would the wolf, who is gentle to everyone, be savage to one woman? What distinguishes her from others? She is no more or less fair, no different in size or – as far as his man's nose can tell – scent. Indeed, the only unusual thing about her is the disappearance of her first husband and the speed with which she married the next.

And that the wolf was found in her lands.

The counsellor goes to the king and finds him remonstrating with the unrepentant wolf. 'Everyone tells me to kill him,' the king says, hopelessly. 'I can't. But what he did… have you seen her face?' he shudders. 'How can I kill my only friend?'

The counsellor, who has long known the king for the lonely man that he is, loyal as ink to paper to the few things that he loves, explains his thoughts. 'It is unlikely that she would confess, my lord,' he says. 'She may need to be asked more…pointedly.'

'Asked what, exactly?' The king ignores his counsellor's implication that they should torture a woman who has just lost her nose. 'You think this lady caused her husband's disappearance – but how? And what has this to do with the wolf?' He drops a protective arm around the wolf's vast shaggy neck, fearing that the animal will be revealed as a man eater, a killer. In that case, he will have no choice.

The counsellor spreads his hands. 'I know not, my lord. But animals, although we wrongly rate them far below us in likeness to God, can neither tell lies nor be taken in by them, whereas we are deceived by little more than a pretty smile.'

The king drops his face to the top of the wolf's head and rubs between the great ears thoughtfully. 'Then let her recover,' he says, 'and put her to the question – though I cannot imagine what that question would be.'

The counsellor bows and leaves the king with his wolf.

Descriptions of torture have no place in a story about wolves and kings. Suffice to say that the torturers are only momentarily nonplussed to find that they cannot not twist her nose, since the lady has already lost it. It takes only a few brief seconds in the iron maiden's embrace before she admits that she has betrayed her husband, who is a bisclavret, by stealing his clothes and condemning him to the loneliness of the forest and the peril of hunters. She gives up her new husband also, and they are both sent into exile and told never to show their disfigured faces again.

There are many things worse than losing lands or life – or even a nose – and it is with great trepidation that the counsellor explains to the king that the wolf he loves is no wolf, but a captive of the wolf's form, who can be changed back by donning the clothes found in his wife's chamber.

What can the king say? What can any of us say when we realize that what is best for the one we love is worst for us? The king sits alone with the wolf all the long afternoon and thinks many things as they watch the red sun fall over the river. He thinks that a king's happiness is always bought dearly. He thinks that he would gladly trade places with the wolf, except that he does not mind being a man so long as he has a friend such as the wolf has been. And he thinks that if he refuses to give the clothes and break the spell, the man would be twice betrayed: once by his wife, and then by his king.

With a heavy heart, the king lays the clothes on the bed, runs a hand over that well-loved head, and leaves the chamber.

When he returns a man is asleep on the royal bed, curled around himself like a wolf or a child. The counsellor gazes on the man with satisfaction, the king with regret, and as the man's eyes open, the wolf within him lies down to sleep.

The Travelling Kiss

Alexander, hoc percipiens magistrum miro modo laudavit, qui eum a morte liberavit. Puellam matri remisit.
Gesta Romanorum

In the throne room at Pataliputra a girl with poison-bright eyes makes a graceful anjali mudra before the king. The king is, of course, Chandragupta Maurya, unifier of India, son-in-law to Seleucus Nicator, one of Alexander's diadochi, and eventual adherent to the Jain faith.

His adviser Chanakya eyes the girl narrowly. He cannot put his finger on her familiarity. He feels his pulse quicken: he sees that the girl is a mirror of himself. At once, he knows who she is and why she has been sent.

The girl, beautiful in that sinuous way of the Nanda women, gets no closer to the king. She leaves in a tinkle of bells from the silver around her ankles, her wrists. She is sent off to Parvataka, a problem minister, with the king's compliments. The girl kisses Parvataka. Her kiss is so toxic that it kills him instantly. Hearing this, Chandragupta touches the feet of his guru, Chanakya.

The story of the poison kiss becomes a play by Vishakhadatta, *The Signet of the Minister.*

The motif of the poison-kiss travels on.

It traces the spine of the Himalayas, crossing the Dasht-e-Lut into Persia. In Persia the kiss lands on the neck of a concubine. In her rooms far from the concubine's quarters, the queen hears screaming, running, shouting for doctors. Her stupid husband has kissed the girl's neck, the queen knows. It is a beautiful neck, ibis-slender and softly envenomed by the queen's own ointment. Foolish king.

But the kiss, having sighed away from the (beheaded) concubine's neck like the stamen from a crocus, flutters through Arabia on a west-

81

blowing wind. Along the way it becomes mingled with the heady name of Alexander; curly-haired, golden Alexander, breaker of horses, founder of cities, student of Aristotle. Aristotle and Alexander have been dead a good half-millennium but a creative, opportunistic Syrian takes the lustre of their names and applies it, like tempera, to a collection of his own letters which he names, irresistibly, *Secretum Secretorum*.

The kiss of the poison-maiden joins a convoy of tales in the Secret of Secrets and travels into Europe. In the cold northern darkness the kiss parts company from the rest of Aristotle's advice, and becomes yet more lethal. Like a tick, the idea of the poison-kiss embeds itself in new stories, new collections, where it is the girl's mere breath that kills, or her bite, her sweat – even her glance. Thus detached from her Indian home and mutated many times in her travels, the poison-maiden is now a consummate killer. Brunetto Latini – trust an Italian! – reveals that the girl had been placed in a snake's egg as a baby, and was mothered with the other hatchlings in the writhing nest. Removed from her ophidian siblings and placed in a cage among people, she could only hiss and weave until she was taught bread and speech. She is so envenomed that a single kiss kills.

Parts of the old stories begin to repeat themselves in new stories. The poison-maiden is sent in marriage to Alexander, and only Aristotle – that scaly, all-observing, infinitely sensitive classifying machine – recognizes a kindred spirit in the girl. He steps up to Alexander. *She has the bearing of snakes*, he says. He proves this by trapping her in a circle of dittany juice, from which no snake can escape. The girl chokes, her hair stands on end, and thus poisoned, the poison-maiden dies herself.

But still, the legend of the kiss travels, even to those dark windy islands at the world's edge, where monks who kiss no one are infected by the poison of the story's strange design. There, it comes to ground again in a new collection which the monks call the *Gesta Romanorum*, between the story of a husband and wife determined to forget one another, and the tale of a priest who drinks of a putrid dead dog. Thus framed, the kiss is used to explain the evils of women, the wisdom of old men, and the obedience of fictional princes.

The queen of the north, the monks write, heard of Alexander's learning. Imagine her, they say, as they clasp earthenware tumblers of warm beer in the refectory, imagine a woman from a northern kingdom, streaks of silver in her hair, the nature of serpents and snow in her heart. She is well-versed in the rule of all cold, wild places: survival is the only thing of interest. Nothing else is worth getting out of your warm bed for.

This woman has a daughter with which she will test Alexander. How can a mother nourish her child on poison? How can she bear to put it between those wet rosebud lips? Listen, brothers – all that matters is the outcome of this disinterested test.

Who knows how the daughter became so beautiful? We're monks! Beauty, officially, comes from prayer, fasting, letting-it-be-done-unto-you-according-to etc, etc. Actual beauty – red-lipped, bright-eyed, fine-figured and steely of purpose – we only think about that privately.

And the girl – what does she think? This girl who has been travelling with the fatal kiss on her pillowy lips for centuries now, killing and being killed in stories told at courts from India to Paris; how does she feel to be some female Achilles – a weapon, a killer, a single-shot gun?

To be honest, brothers, who cares? Objects don't feel. The knife does not cry, nor does the gun regret. This is the nature of stories which travel fast and light: they reduce everyone to a function, too sparsely-drawn for feelings. At best, the girl accepts that she has a purpose.

And off she goes, fed and fuelled for this end – her whole life constricting to a moment. She has spent years imagining it: moving into Alexander's sphere of warmth, coming towards him, crossing the border into the frisson zone where you must close your eyes, relax your lips, and let crease meet crease. So many years, so much poison eaten, one life consigned to one task – no wonder we preach that mankind is broken, right down to the marrow.

But it has all been seen ahead of time by the old man who stands at the prince's elbow. Imagine the poison-maiden's confusion when she understands that Alexander is a ventriloquist's dummy. He is as much a mere pair of lips as she! And that Aristotle, that dry categorizer of men and things, is the real speaker. It is through the lips of the king's tutor that the order to avoid her comes. Aristotle, brothers, kisses no one.

And what about the feelings of the prisoner who is brought in, quaking and stupefied that this is how he will die – at the hand of a mere girl? Alexander sulks in the corner because he has been forbidden the tainted northern sweetmeat.

Enthroned, the girl receives the prisoner's trembling kiss, his whole sweating body shaking like half-set aspic. And then she watches the poor sod convulse, sweat, gasp, expire. Better not to think of the feelings of the hapless kiss-taster. There is no beheading of the girl: she and her labial armoury are returned, depleted of poison, with Alexander's compliments.

The kiss-motif retreats with her to its northern fastness and does not reappear for some four centuries, until it is blown to the New World.

From the body, to the body narrative, to the body digital, the poison-kiss is still travelling.

Floating Man

One of us must suppose that he was just created at a stroke, fully developed and perfectly formed but with his vision shrouded...

Ibn Sina, *Al-Ishārāt wa-al-Tanbīhāt* (Directives and Reminders)

The Floating Man has come to earth. A few minutes ago, he descended from his thousand-year drift in the exosphere and landed in a suburbanfront garden. A mother is about to take her teenage daughter to school when they come upon him, this mental figment belonging to Abu 'Ali al-Husayn ibn 'Abd Allah ibn Al-Hasan ibn Alli ibn Sina, whom you may know as Avicenna. And this is where the story begins.

Stories have a beginning, a middle and an end. But these things are only apparent if you know about time. Time is only apparent if you have a body.

For the first time, the Floating Man feels this sensation, of having a body. Soon, it will make him understand time. How soon? Around five minutes, to us. But who can say what that interval feels like to him? Imagine the first five-minute span of which you were ever aware. Your mind, until now adrift in a plain of abstraction as limitless as any Euclidean space, now feels moments, scudding on the smooth surface of continuous thought, like pockets of turbulence beneath an aircraft.

Time sticks, like millions of little adhesions, to the Floating Man's mind. For the first time, his thinking (which is to say his whole being) staggers under the weight of them.

Then something even bigger dawns on him. It is this: that there is first one thing *and then* another. And then he notices that these moments, these pockets of turbulence, are linear. There is a flow of them and it is impossible to go against the flow. You move onward, always leaving something behind, unable to go back.

In this first five minutes on earth, in someone's front garden, the Floating Man has become aware of time, and change, and loss. And none of this even takes into account the astonishing sensation of *things*, material things, all around him, coming into contact with the body he has only just discovered that he has. The body, he will soon find out, that he *is*.

You see, until now he has only been a Floating Man, a homunculus in Avicenna's thought-experiment, blissfully drifting on the plane of the page, in the darkness of Avicenna's capacious brain. There, according to the philosopher, he drifted unseeing, unhearing, unsmelling, his limbs not touching any other part of his body. And all of this has been in aid of a mighty point, to which the eleventh century bowed: that the mind could know itself without the help of the body. And that this holy communion of mind and reflected mind – this self-knowledge was the soul itself, immaterial, immortal, intransient.

But now the Floating Man has descended to earth and finds himself in the meat-box of a body. It is like being born, pushed out of the drifting warmth and dropped, still sleepy and blissful, into a world of light, angles, voices.

'I think we should phone the police.'

'He's just drunk. Or something. Sorry, excuse me – *'Scuse me*!' There is a new feeling on the gelid layer he will come to know as his skin. A sudden intense pressure, then nothing. He recoils within himself at the feeling. It is more than the sensation of the prickling grass beneath his bare legs. It comes from the moving shape, the noisy thing which blocks out the sun. The shape controls this pressure on his new skin. He will come to know this as pain.

'You can't be here. This is private property. Do you understand – do you think he speaks English? There –' and the shape changes. A long thing, an arm (he has one too, he sees), extends itself and tapers to a point. It is a finger. He has those. He looks at his fingers. He has a thought. *I have what this other being has. These fingers. We are alike. But I am I-who-has-fingers and the Other is Other-who-has-fingers.*

'—that's the boundary of this property; *our* property. This is *our* garden, see? See? Our house.'

He practises raising his arm, like her. Suddenly there is distance between them.

'Now, you don't have to… Can you put your hand down, then?'

It turns away and the sound recedes a bit. 'No, not your father. He's at work. Yes, just call them here – here's my phone – they'll come quickly if they know we're on our own.'

He shows her his fingers. *We are alike. I have these, too.* He moves the hand through the air, feeling the breeze on the sides of his fingers, seeing the sun glint between them.

'What happened to your clothes? Have you been hurt? You should be…you can't just be *sleeping* in someone's garden, naked like this. I mean…for God's sake, did you get through to them?'

He turns his head – so heavy, this huge weight at the top of him! He sees the blue sky above them. He feels its pull, knows somehow that this is where he has come from. He feels provenance. Soon, this will merge with the understanding of distance. He will know longing.

'Are they coming? Get a blanket or something – no, not that one. Because it's cashmere! There're some raggedy ones in the garage. Your dad uses them for the – oh, thank God. Here they are. Hello! We're just here!'

He sees more two-legged things coming towards them, darkly dressed, emitting a deeper burble of sound. He notices their common form. He holds his arms out – *I have these, like you. We are all alike.*

'Yes, just here, like this. Asleep. I have no idea where he's come from.'

He tries to touch one of the dark figures, stretching his hand out to them. *I am me. I am in this cladding of skin. Are you within yours? Were you once floating like me? Direct the noise you make to me. Include me. Include me.*

And there is a sudden snap and a cold hardness around his wrists, two circular things which shine brightly. Puzzled, he stares at his hands, which are now trapped at a fixed distance from each other.

Five minutes have passed. He knows that he cannot change this new feeling for the previous one. He knows what time is now, and it has noticed him. As he is led away the Floating Man understands what he was, and what he is now, and that it is not the same.

A Theft

...dum puelle se movendo
gestibus lasciviunt,
asto videns, et videndo
me michi subripiunt.
Carmina Burana 75

Having never possessed any items of great value, I've never had anything significant stolen. Those little things which went astray (or *got lifted, to* use a Glasgow expression), only ever occasioned a mild annoyance. The only things which can really be stolen, in the sense of something taken away with effort and daring and provoking real outrage, are the intrinsic things: your time, your hopes, happiness, your health. Who hasn't had jobs that have stolen their time? Friendships and relationships that made off with your hopes, or horrible surprises that took your happiness like a pocket-picker in a coffee-shop? How many people have had their health stolen by the bent bookmaker that is society? And yet, the need to keep going, even when you're beset by bandits of chance, opportunity, and vindictiveness, says that we should respond to those thefts with the same kind of amused disbelief that you feel when you find that someone has nicked a gym-bag full of sweaty kit. Amused disbelief because you see how easily you come apart; because the theft is so lightly achieved; because the thief, sometimes, is so beautiful.

This experience is most beautifully described in a poem of the German Middle Ages, in which a student looks at the dancing girls whom he loves and can't have, those beautiful thieves *se movendo gestibus lasciviunt, adsto videns et videndo me mihi surripiunt.*

Fair Rosaline

She hath forsworn to love, and in that vow
Do I live dead that live to tell it now.
William Shakespeare, *Romeo and Juliet*

Rosaline woke to the silence. She didn't like Romeo's singing, but she disliked its absence more. She was well aware that her treatment of his had gained her the name of a crow, but what was she supposed to do? Despite being as Florentine as the Arno, she had no time or patience for bargaining – particularly not over something as trivial as chastity. It was easier to say she was sworn to chastity and let him pine away under her window. She had been good enough to shove a mask at him when he crashed her uncle's party, and made sure he got away unscathed. Even if it was looking like Tartoglio.

She lay back in bed and tried to ignore her nurse's snoring. The nurse would wake soon and lament Romeo's absence and harp on at the virtues of Juliet, Rosaline's pretty but dim-witted younger cousin. The nurse had insisted that Juliet had caught Romeo's eye at the same party.

It wasn't that Rosaline minded losing Romeo to Juliet, who would then have to navigate the byzantine feud between their houses. It was that she minded losing. She was already looked on as a rather dour case, but this put her on the shelf of once-was and also-ran girls, and she resented that.

She knew almost exactly how it would all play out for them both, and was therefore very glad to have kept the little bottle of belladonna on which she had relied to take the edge off Romeo's singing. Even friars and nurses commit indiscretions and can be controlled by those who have knowledge of them. She was saving Juliet from the miseries of marriage and childbed, and Romeo from the delusion of musical talent.

A Tempest

Prospero: *It goes on, I see,*
As my soul prompts it.
William Shakespeare, *The Tempest*

Weeping, grieving, Ferdinand sits on the sand facing the crashing ocean. He remembers talking about this situation with his tutor: if a man finds himself alone, the last soul on earth, ruler of a kingdom of one, is it still incumbent on him to act virtuously? Can he, in fact, act otherwise? Dazed, he recalls his tutor saying that vice was not a product of other men's society.

How long he cries for, he can't quite say. At least the length of the song, a weird, nasal sound like a jew's harp. He should be startled by this music, which mocks his dead father as no more than fish food, but he accepts that it's a hallucination of his grief-disordered brain.

By and bye he stands, princely on the yellow sands, the lost heir-apparent to a mislaid kingdom. East and west the beach stretches, and behind him a treeline such as has been described by travellers to the New World. But this is the little Mediterranean, the sea at the world's centre. Civilization itself has been bathed here as a baby. Although the horizon is blue and final, he knows that ships will pass. All he must do to be rescued is keep a fire going on the beach and wait for the smoke to be seen. He can fish a little; he knows how to make a shelter from fronds. Delicate flowers in the grass suggest fresh water somewhere. He will wait to be discovered.

A sneaking gladness creeps into his heart. He suspects that he has the best of all worlds here – provided he's discovered fairly soon. Grief for his father withdraws a little. The music fades. He stares at the sea with less apprehension.

Resolved, he turns. To the east, a black spot hovers on the sand far down the beach. His first thought is a bear, but it moves with the dignity of a man. A man's measured cadence, neither running nor staggering. It is not one of the sailors, Ferdinand is sure. Fearing that it portends an attack, he scans the treeline. And finds nothing. But to the west, advancing upon him from the other side, is a bigger spot, a blueish macula blurring at high speed along the sand.

What will he do? Alone, unarmed, unheralded, Ferdinand is a castaway on a nameless island. The inhabitants may know or care nothing of Milan or his high breeding. He is reduced to basic weapons: truth, courtesy, the hope for discovery. He looks within himself and discovers that it has been some time since he polished these.

All he can do is wait. It strikes him that this may be how the soul feels after death. Alone on a wide strand, the ocean of life crashing before him, his little barque now sunk. Advanced upon from both sides by forces he cannot know. And he, friendless, reduced to courtesy and pleading.

The eastward shape is closer now, much closer. Ferdinand discerns the nobility of human proportions. Long, slender, strong legs. A proportionate torso from which hang elegant arms. A head, large-seeming at this distance. Dark in hue, all of it, though this may be the sun.

Quickly, he looks at the westward figure, the larger, faster one. It has broken apart; Ferdinand sees two figures, skimming the sands towards him. The size is attributable to a vast blue cloak, cerulean, snapping and rippling behind one figure. The other is reed-like, but golden, or so it seems. There is something determined, almost predatory, about their approach. He fears.

The eastward figure is revealed: a young man of Ferdinand's age, gleaming black and perfect, his hair in a waterfall of thick locks hanging from a rolled crown of hair like a garland around his head. He wears only a tattered clout about his waist, but this reveals a form built for speed and strength; the elegance of a hunter, the restrained decorum of a dancer. He raises a hand as he approaches Ferdinand, holding it out with a broad and brilliant smile. Astounded by the youth's beauty, Ferdinand is transported with a kind of high delight.

They face each other, eye to eye. 'My very other self,' Ferdinand says, looking gladly at the boy's dark beauty. 'A counterpart in ink to my pale paper. I, who was a prince, a son, put-upon ruler of a vanished kingdom, have discovered my obverse on this distant shore. On this golden strand I am made a king, a bridegroom, a subject, even as a castaway.'

Discovering that the golden youth speaks like himself, the sable mirror laughs. 'So must the world have been when it was young,' says Ferdinand, passing a curious hand over the youth's shoulders, thenecklace of blazing feathers and threaded seeds, 'when night and day came together before the waters, and that happy pair had the naming of the birds and beasts before them.'

The dark boy touches Ferdinand's blonde curls, murmuring something which sounds like birds in the forest. Ferdinand, his heart shipwrecked by love, is charmed from moving. 'Are you made or no?' he whispers. 'What chance delivered you, thus unsullied, from a mother's fetid grasp? Or are you elemental, man's lost virtue living here, undiscovered by kings and commonwealths whose reigns drag them further from perfection?'

The boy places a hand over Ferdinand's moving lips and gently draws him to his side. Thus united, they stand on the sands shoulder to shoulder, as the imperious magician and his golden-haired honey-trap bear down on them.

The Chiding

So, when this loose behavior I throw off
And pay the debt I never promised,
By how much better than my word I am,
By so much shall I falsify men's hopes
William Shakespeare, *Henry IV, Part I*

Father turfed the council out and went to town on Hal. I suppose it was for the sake of Hal's blasted dignity that he booted us all out, but you could still hear him from the garden.

It might have been more prudent for them both to have been quieter – who, really, wants to hear their father divulge the shabby secrets of his constructed majesty? Who wants to hear the man they backed – to the point of regicide – explain to his successor how to keep up the façade? Who, of all the second sons, the world's afterthoughts, wants to hear a king exhort his heir to uphold the promise of their house? A house which is mostly built on sand, and a king who took the crown like a kitchen knave finding a pie on a table. No wonder Pa goes on about how ill Hal's head fits the crown, since the crown was neither bequeathed nor won in fair fight.

Pa is dying, Hal is a knave, Tom a child, and I – I am no more than the replacement for my princely brother on the council. But I am mentioned with approval by Pa, if only to chide the rightwise occupant of that seat.

My entire life has been a story of gifts given left-handed. The second son of a usurping king. The stalwart dull brother of a larking boy who will one day make me bow to him. A stop-gap, also-ran, fall-back, whatever-you-will nobody who does what he's told and clears out when it's unseemly.

I should pity Hal, I suppose. We're no more friends than any heir and his understudy could ever be, but he said once that he'd rather have stayed with our uncle in Oxford, or be a kitchen boy in the Eastcheap stews, than shoulder the legend of father's hasty and dubious kingship. I hushed him up, but he was in a passion and railed about unpromised debts and the chains of other men's quarrels. Not the time to have told him that I'd have the crown if he didn't want it. It's never the time to say that. It's not a thing that can be said, anyway. Father never did, even when Richard was at his flighty worst. He just let it be known, silently, pervasively, like a mist on the marshes, that he'd do better with the crown than Richard – or Mortimer, who now haunts him and is the ache that he calls arthritis.

And so it happened. I have no confidence in Providence, however well it has treated Pa and Hal. I'm neither glorious nor abysmal, neither Percy nor Prince of Wales, neither fish nor fowl. Forgettable. And while it means that I'll never be railed as at Hal was – no one will ever extort promises from me like those Hal made about seeing off Hotspur – I'll never be required to fulfil them, either.

No one would dream of doughy Lancaster idling away the glory of his princely blood by taverning or wenching. No father would rather have some other John, some better-made double from another cradle, with keener blood and a mettle that fires a father's heart. Sometimes Pa forgets I'm even his son – when he looks around that table of greybeards and counts me – obedient, resigned, loyal – among them. It's hardly the place to ask him if he ever loved me, John, not Lancaster, not the councillor-who-is-not-Hal, but me, even a little.

So Hal made his promises and father stopped roaring and the clerks and kitchen maids, the ostlers and yeomen, all breathed out again. Hal beat a retreat to the stews to collect what was left of his dignity and a company, and we are all sent to Shrewsbury to put paid to the Percies and their better sons.

Hal will fight Hotspur and he will win. Hotspur – older, bolder, better in arms, just in his cause, noble in his bearing – will fall to Hal's untutored sword because Providence smiles on Hal, not Hotspur. You can feel it, even as Hal acts the common brigand, even as he shakes off the sack in which he washes his face. Like the heat of a long-promised summer, Hal will lightly overleap those hurdles which should justly pull him down.

And it makes me sick.

On this kiss

'Is it you, my Prince?' she said. 'You have been a long while coming!'
Arthur Quiller-Couch, *The Sleeping Beauty*

She smelled of leaf mulch and cold. It wasn't a body smell at all, about which Gerald was relieved. He'd been expecting the smell of decay - not that he knew what human decay smelt like, but he'd caught a whiff of bad meat once, walking past a butcher's shop, and imagined it was something like that.

Saying 'he'd been expecting' makes it sound as though Gerald had thought about it for a long time, which isn't quite true. He'd seen the body a few minutes previously, when he came into the clearing and found her lying under the bare trees, the last leaves of autumn drifting down into her hair.

He would have been ashamed if anyone had seen his lack of concern. But he'd parked concern about other people's opinions back on the road with his car. He felt as he always felt when he was alone in the woods, absolutely sure of a few things, the only things that concerned him. He supposed it was what Thoreau had meant by living deliberately. Somehow, it meant that finding a random corpse in the woods didn't feel surprising. It also meant that he was sure he would kiss her.

He approached her unhurriedly. He didn't look around to see if he was alone. Only people with a guilty conscience do that and - although it might seem creepy, and although random men alone in the woods kissing stone-cold girls under trees might seem guilty of something to *us* - he certainly didn't feel guilty of anything.

He wasn't a rapist, a stalker, a survivalist, or even a naturist. He just liked being alone in the quiet woods with his dog, who was off somewhere scaring things in the undergrowth. He saw a girl under a tree. He knew what girls were, and trees. He knew that people die. Put those three known things together and it's perfectly rational not to fuss when you come across a dead girl under a tree. The kiss, I grant you, doesn't fit with all of that, but you cannot tell children fairy tales and not expect unusual results.

But as he walks across the clearing, feeling the thick carpet of leaves bounce and sigh under his weight, with autumn all around him, he was more than just Gerald-who-has-a-dog-and-a-duplex. He was a man alone in the woods, where men are princes or huntsmen, royal messengers, or outlaws subject only to the laws of the seasons. Women, by the same logic, are princesses, little girls lost, or witches.

So he stands looking down at her, wondering how long she's been there. He knows, with the same certainty that he knows evening will fall, that he'll kiss her. Secretly, he also feels slightly squeamish at the thought that maggots may be fattening themselves on her decaying sweetness. So he kneels down and smells her first, cautiously, like a dog.

He notices how fine her red-gold hair is, strewn among the leaves. He remembers a poem he read about a knight 'with red-gold glamour, a knight in the wheat', and it makes sense now. He brushes a finger over the collar of her woollen sweater, which is dark blue, and made of very fine wool. Her legs are bent slightly, like a sleeper's, and her brown leather hiking boots are new. He sniffs again, but all he smells is cold and the great forests of the Pacific northwest.

She looks like many young women with red gold hair. Fine-boned, a light scatter of auburn freckles across her face, an elegant mouth with unchapped lips and the finest tracery of lines beginning to show around it. It's impossible to get a sense of someone when they're asleep.

He cocks his head this way and that, trying to work out what the best angle of approach is. There are a few rocks scattered on the other side of her, which would be in the way if he moved to the other, more convenient, side. He leans right over and steadies himself with a hand on either side of her head.

And kisses her.

So we have a man in the woods kissing a dead girl that he's found lying beneath a tree. It's not intended to be the kiss of life, but it might as well be. Underneath the soft pressure of his lips, she draws a great breath, like a sigh, and opens her eyes.

'What are you doing?'

He rocks back on his heels and stares at her for a second, feeling the shockwave of their mutually exclusive fairy tales clash and eddy. From his perspective, this bit *is* unexpected. And disquieting. It feels like a scab being pulled away from a wound. The scab is Gerald-with-a-dog-and-duplex, and the wound is Gerald-alone-in-the-woods. This explains why he takes one of the rocks and beats her over the head with it.

He doesn't see whether she's dead (again) or not. He whistles for the dog, walks back up to the road with the rock in his hand, and shuts the car door as a sense of evening seeps coldly into the air.

Are you disappointed? What sort of denouement can there be for this brief glimpse of an event which probably happens quite often? Don't forget - keen readers heartily endorse this whole kissing-in-the-woods. Without that drive which makes a young man in the woods kiss some beautiful but entirely random dead girl, we would have no fairy tales. Whether he marries her or murders her is immaterial. That comes after the kiss, for which we cannot chastise him without getting rid of men altogether. Events, which are individual, are different to drives, which are universal. It's hardly a horror story, this. On this kiss in the woods is built all our happily ever afters.

Spindle

"But what sort of linen," said they, "would His Majesty have us spin without spindles?"

Arthur Quiller-Couch, *The Sleeping Beauty*

When I explained that a spindle is sharp, the constable looked up from her notebook and said, 'So it could be used as a weapon?'

I said, 'Well, I suppose so. But so could a knitting needle. Or a teaspoon, for that matter.'

She gave me a look I've spent my life getting: a my-time-is-precious-don't-be-funny-with-me look. She closed the notebook with a snap. 'OK, we've got her description. I'm around here for the rest of the afternoon. If we see her we'll stop her and maybe bring her in and you can identify her.' She was already turning away as she said it.

I watched her close the door and thought that, once upon a time a young woman like her would have been rated by the yarn she produced with a spindle. Or maybe not. Maybe she would always have been the equivalent of a constable. The village prefect. The kind of woman who sorted out wife-beaters and gossips, led the hue and cry and stared down the magistrate until he handed out an appropriate sentence.

She came back the week before Christmas. 'Hello again,' she said. She put five small embroidery kits on the counter. I'd forgotten who she was. 'The case of the stolen spindle,' she said.

'Yes!' I said. 'Silly of me. I didn't recognize you in mufti. Have you started embroidery?'

'Nieces,' she said briefly. 'Five nieces, one nephew. I'm better on his presents, but I think these'll make my sisters happy.'

'How many sisters?'

'Two,' she said. 'I'm the eldest.'

'Me too.' We smiled at each other for a moment, the shared smile of things that only eldest children know about. Believe me, it matters. 'Did you ever find the girl with that spindle?' I said, starting to ring up the kits.

'Actually, we did,' she said, looking for her wallet. I noticed a faint blush on her neck. I wondered if she was embarrassed about not telling me. I'd just have lied and said no. Fleetingly, I caught a glimpse inside her world. Her own personal curse, always telling the truth. Like Cassandra in a stab vest.

'It wouldn't be worth your while pressing charges, you know,' she said, slightly defensively. 'That's why I didn't bother you with it.'

'No,' I said hurriedly, 'it wasn't that. I just wondered if she was, you know, alright. If there was something I could do to help. I'm not such a hard-bitten businesswoman that I'd see someone suffer for the sake of a spindle.'

'Oh.' Her shoulders dropped a little. 'She had... you know... mental health issues. We caught her in the shopping centre stealing a kid's red coat. She didn't even have any kids. We took her in and the magistrate gave her community service and a mandatory mental health assessment. I saw her the other day, just sitting on the swings in the Harwood Estate. Don't worry though. I doubt she'll be back in here.'

I put the kits in a bag. 'It wasn't that. I wondered if maybe she'd like to come in and learn to spin with the spindle.'

She gave me a similar look to the one from months before, but a softened version this time. Don't waste *your* time instead of don't waste *my* time. 'Yeah, well, far be it from me to ...'

'...rain on my good deeds' parade?' I said wryly. 'I know what you're saying. But imagine if it did some good. You may say I'm a dreamer—'

'But I'm not the only one.' She sang it, in a surprisingly light voice. A girl's voice, not a woman in her thirties.

'Pretty voice.' There was an embarrassed smile between us. She took the bag.

'Let me know how it goes, if you do,' she said. 'And be careful.'

'I will,' I said. 'Come back in. I'll even start you on your own embroidery.' She laughed and was gone again. I still didn't know her name.

I walked to the Harwood Estate the next day after closing. The council Christmas lights vanished and the estate closed in around the street. Even the buses shot through as if they were in a war zone. Despite the dark and cold a couple of teenagers were sitting listlessly on the swings. They sized me up and decided I had nothing worth taking. I pulled my duffel coat closer and went over to them.

'Do you know a girl, about twenty, long dark hair? She sometimes sits on these swings?'

'What kina gel?' One of the boys affected a Jamaican accent, mixed with Brixton. He had toffee-coloured skin and beautiful, precisely-shaped ears.

'What do you mean?'

He gave the suck-tut noise of irritation which can mean everything from a condemnation of your intelligence to an invitation to oral sex. 'What colour she, like?'

'Oh right. White. Like me,' I said, unneccesarily.

The other boy, who had astonishing, lupine-golden eyes, hit his friend briefly. 'She mean dat crazy gel. You know, the one lives two down from Nige's aunty.' He turned to the monolith of the first building, and pointed to a single window where a very dim glow shone, six floors up, behind an exterior walkway. 'I think that's her. She had some troubles years back. Dad died and she got lef' with her stepmother. Mean cow she was.'

I thanked them and walked over to the building. Behind a skip was a single entrance to the stairwell. From forty feet away it reeked of skunk and urine and cheap body spray. I put my head inside the doorway but, repelled by the stench and the darkness, withdrew.

I stood in the pallid glow of a streetlight, considering. What was I really doing here, not even knowing the girl's name – a girl with mental health issues who had shoplifted from me? Whose fairy godmother was I pretending to be, lurking here at the entrance to London's equivalent of the dark forest? A small voice reminded me of the dangers of trying to save anyone.

I realized that dithering in front of the building was more likely to bring trouble than just forging ahead, so I went into the stairwell, holding my breath and wishing I had a torch. Small things skittered and scratched and I could feel an assortment of cans, crisp packets and light tubular things which felt like needles. I slipped on something like cardboard and staggered, my hand finding the wall and just as quickly jerking away from it. I was afraid of stepping on a body, living or otherwise. I thought about the wolf eyes of the boy on the swings and what else might be in the next five flights of squelching, stinking darkness.

Just as quickly it came to me: *this is where she lives.* This threw a frame around the girl's entire existence. Stranded between the London sky and the street, up six floors of dank trash, one cage in a run of predators. Of everything she could have stolen, why did she steal a spindle? Why did she steal it from me?

Wheezing slightly from the mouth-breathing I had done, I got to the sixth floor and stopped to get my bearings again. The window to which the boy had pointed was at the end of a long gallery, tacked onto the exterior of the tower. A fine rain was falling, but I was above the streetlights, so the long needles were only lit by the ambient buzz of London light pollution. I set off down the gallery, kicking aside some sweetly rotting garbage every few steps.

Noise and cooking smells leeched out of most front doors and hung like invisible vestibules along the walkway. Some windows had Christmas decorations, from the tasteful to *Merry Xmas, Now Fuck Off* in flashing red. Only her door was still, silent, untainted by the smell of life, the window undecorated. There was a glow behind the safety glass that suggested either a television on bluescreen, or a blue lamp, far from the door.

Tentatively, I clapped the letter box in the absence of a knocker or doorbell. I sensed, more than heard, a tiny movement deep within the flat. There was a long moment which felt like a wheel, rapidly unwinding something, and I knocked again.

It's hard to say when the rules of a game become clear to you. A penny dropped and I understood that she would not, could not, come to the door. I pushed gently and it opened with a click onto a small, dark hall, with a tiny radiator emitting no heat. A living room, curtained and unlit, came off the hall. The shapes of a sofa and small table, a hard chair and a bookcase.

I became aware of the girl, sitting motionless on the floor near the window, at the same time as I drew in a breath of the place and registered the air she lived in. I'm good with two things: needlecraft and smells. I'm told it's not actually a talent of the nose – I don't smell any more keenly than anyone else – but rather of the brain. My brain remembers smells better, and somehow, I draw more accurate conclusions about the situations I smell.

It smelled private. There was a stale smell of old, cheap carpeting twinned with a deep cold, the cold of indoors, of frigid still places and bad diets, of restlessness and close-packed humans and dirt. There was also the smell peculiar to tears, or perhaps it's the smell of the sweat that comes with hard and prolonged crying. And books. Several hundred, possibly a thousand books, each with their own particular scent and age, weight, handle, and fingering. I couldn't see them, but the smell was easily many times that of a second-hand bookshop.

'Hello?' I stopped just inside the living room doorway. I was unwilling to go further into a room where I couldn't see the floor. There was a movement from somewhere ahead of me.

'What do you want?' Her voice was tiny. Exhausted as a sparrow. She sounded entirely without fear or expectation.

'Do you mind if I turn a light on? I don't want to trip over.'

'Can't. No power.'

That took away the next few things I'd planned to say. 'You may not remember, but you were in my shop a few weeks ago. Skimbleshanks? It's off the Marylebone Road. I sell wool. Spinning things.'

'Yeah.'

'Look, I'm going to use my phone for some light. I can't have a conversation with a total stranger in the dark.'

I fumbled in my bag and produced my phone, then held it in front of me like a witch with her wand. A blue rectangle which only illuminated my thumb appeared at the end of my arm. I turned the phone around and saw her outline beneath the curtained window. The curtain was too short, and a bright band of city night fell on a face that seemed mostly eyes.

The floor was clear, so I walked gingerly ahead to the window and crouched down by her. She wore a puffy parka like the ones the long-term homeless and well-heeled gap-year kids wear. Uncomfortably, I settled cross-legged in front of her, dragging my boots under each corduroy knee. She looked at me without interest. The relaxing thing about people who have hit the absolute bottom is that you can take your time. I guessed that she had already heard everything that began with *we're concerned about you* and used the words *managing* or *management*.

It seemed fairly clear that, sitting on the cold carpet beneath the window, she was waiting for death like someone waiting for a taxi with its light on.

'You took a spindle from my shop.'

Something tiny and fleeting crossed her face. Actually, it made her look worse, like opening a curtain in a hoarder's house. She put a hand in her pocket and brought out the spindle. She offered it on an open palm on which several deep, straight cuts looked like pen streaks in the dimness.

'I don't want it back. I just wondered what you wanted it for.'

She looked down and dropped her hand. The spindle rolled onto the carpet. She shrugged. Nothing annoys me as much as a shrug. Keeping to myself is how I've lived. It's not a boast, just a way of saying that if there's a dispute it is very rarely me who has started it. I don't mind an argument, but I resent being drawn out and left with my dander up because apathy has overcome someone.

'That's not an answer. Come on, what did you want with the spindle?' I think the demand took her by surprise. I've noticed that people with a 'condition' or the loathsome anodyne 'issues' of official services never have any demands put to them. They are managed into situations like bulky bits of furniture and told things about themselves by way of an explanation. There may be a question mark at the end of these things; there may not.

The magic of a question is that it binds another person into an event. If you don't answer, you're holding things up. You become the ringmaster of that pause. If you answer, you own the next pitch of the conversation. A question throws a spell around another person, like a spancel.

'Just wanted it.'

'Why? Can you spin?'

Her face briefly transformed into a rictus, another awful flash of exhaustion. 'No.'

'Did you know what it was?'

'Yeah.'

'Most people wouldn't.' It was like performing CPR. Keeping up a constant, exhausting pressure of words until I felt an answering thump. 'So you know what a spindle is but not how to use it? Where did you learn what it was?'

'Book.'

'Spinning book?'

'Fairy tale book.'

'So you took the spindle because you thought you'd prick your finger on it and what, sleep? Be rescued by a prince?'

There was a dreadful pause, full of ice, shining with certainty, the slightly vibrant moment where some nail has been struck resoundingly on the head. Very slowly, she leaned her head against the wall and closed her eyes. Her cheeks dropped into hollows. 'Laugh and go away.'

'I'm not laughing. I sell spindles. Why would I laugh at the most important story about one?'

'Because it's stupid. I'm stupid.'

'Maybe, but not about the spindle. After all, it brought me here. I'm not quite a prince, but I can't help that.'

'Can you make me sleep a hundred years then?'

'Probably not, unless I start talking about trying to run a small business in north London.'

She opened her eyes and looked at me, still on the diagonal, against the wall. She reminded me of a rescue cat I'd had once. It was past wary. It cared nothing for anyone, whether it got hurt or not, and would lash out with a clawful of knives until you left it alone. The only time it voluntarily came to me it turned out to have a brain tumour pressing against the back of one eye, and was asking me to help it die.

'I don't blame you for hoping that the spindle magic would work. I don't even blame you for stealing the spindle.'

The light from the window above her sent a wash of frosty grey down her face like a mask of sleet. Making it up as I went along, I said, 'I blame you for trying to use a thing you don't understand. There's magic in a spindle, but you have to earn it. Weaving, spinning, it takes years to master. *Then* the tools are yours to summon up whatever you want with. And I think that, properly used, a prince is the very least of what you could call.'

'What are you saying? Learn to spin? Who'll teach me – you? And that'll sort out all my problems?' She was absolutely still beneath the window.

107

'Of course not. I can't sort out your problems. But I can teach you to spin, and you can pay me by minding the shop instead of stealing from it.'

I saw a flurry of things fight behind her eyes. 'I don't…I can't leave this…'

'Yes you can,' I said, more briskly than I felt. 'Come home with me now, and we'll get started.'

She lifted her head from the wall. 'What, now?'

'Got something else to do?' I felt myself getting up, stiff as a dowel in the cold, putting a hand on the puffy sleeve and grasping for her wrist inside it. She gave a yelp. I pushed back the rustling sleeve. Her wrist, like an ivory cuff, had a red circle, braceleted about the bone.

I pulled down the sleeve and took her hand, pulling her up. She was about my height, and a long rope of dark hair uncoiled and snaked down one shoulder, mirroring my own. We stood for a moment being each other's mirror before I laughed.

'I'm afraid of going back down that stairwell.'

She gave a twitch that might become a smile. "S just dark. Dark and stink. There's worse things than that stairwell.'

'Let's avoid them too, then.'

I don't recall whether we locked her door, but she held my hand all the way out of the tower.

From the Greater London Record Office

DLC/310, folios 19-20

And there she voluntarily confessed
That she had long frequented all
(or most) of the disorderly
and licentious places in this city
as namely she hath usually
in the habit of a man resorted
to alehouses, taverns, tobacco shops
and also to playhouses

> (there is an ellipsis here, and in it
> is this whole woman's fall or redemption,
> for it could have been filled with
> nunneries, poor-houses, the dwellings of the sick
> the split lips of beaten wives
> the agonies of the dying
> the wet cloth pressed lovingly to the helpless hot brow
> but rather it elides, as she is accused of doing)

and namely (it goes on) being
at a play about three-quarters
of a year (not three-quarters of her
for she seems pretty indivisible
and anyway, what's a quarter of a woman but a man)
since at the Fortune (and since is causal, not temporal)
in man's apparel, and in her boots,
and with a sword by her side,
she told the company there present
that she thought many of them were of the opinion
> (note the difference)
that she was a man, but if

any of them were to come to her lodging
they should find that she is a woman
and some other immodest and lascivious speeches
she also used at that time.

    (But imagine what speeches she used at other times
    how tender, her amber liquid speech on private walls
    how monstrous her loneliness in the world, how charitable)

and also sat there upon the stage
in the public view of all the people
there present (their present)
in man's apparel
and played upon her lute
and sang a song.

Fable

Nasi-ga-ri

Notebooks of Lt. William Dawes, RN, 1788

CAST

WILLIAM DAWES, once astronomer to the First Fleet in Sydney, now governor of the colony of Sierra Leone

PATYEGARANG, an Eora woman who taught Dawes the rudiments of the Eora language spoken in the Sydney Cove area

CHILDREN of the Sierra Leone settlement. (These are optional – Dawes can simply speak to seats in the schoolroom if necessary).

Freetown, Sierra Leone, 1792. A whitewashed schoolroom, with a class of small black children being taught by a white man. DAWES *looks exhausted, abstracted and unhappy. The children have primers open to a page of fables.*

DAWES: Let us read, then. It is a fable. A slave owner tried to wash his black slave white but found that the blackness was in the skin. Do you understand? This is a fable. The exercise is to amplify it. Amplify – make it greater. Yes, like this. Fatter, yes! Exactly, like a fat man – well done. I shall do an example, to show you. I recall a time, in Semicircular Quay, in the Colony of New South Wales, in 1788. Yes, before you were all born.

[*The lights dim until only a spotlight is on* DAWES. PATYE, *around sixteen years old, brings a washing tub and clothes into the spotlight, settles on the floor and begins to rub the clothes, working in the water and soap.*]

She sits before the tub.

PATYE: *He rub cloes wit soak*

DAWES: Rubs. He rubs the clothes with the soap.

111

PATYE: *He rub rubs man with soap.*

DAWES: Man? What man?

PATYE: *You. Mester Dawesman.*

DAWES: He rubs himself with the soap. But we say 'wash'. Sh—washshshsh. He washes himself with soap. He washes himself with the soap.

PATYE: *Yes. They cloes clean.*

DAWES: The clothes become clean. I should think they do, with all the scrubbing.

PATYE: *Skrubbing.*

DAWES: Scrrrrrubbbb, you know, rub very hard. Like this—skrubbbb-bub-bub-bub-ing!

PATYE: *skrubbbb-bub-bub-bub-ing!*

DAWES: Now Patye is scrubbed. Now Patye is clean.

PATYE: *Patye not clean.*

DAWES: How so?

PATYE: *Patye old cloes. Patye Skrubby.*

DAWES: Scrubby? Oh, a stain. Why do you think you're like the stain? Yes, but your skin is black. My skin is white. See, Patye black clean, Dawes white clean. Same.

PATYE: *No. No. Patye like Dawes clean.*

DAWES: I'm glad you like me clean! But you are clean. Look –wait—
where are you going? Patye, you can't wash it off! Come back here!

PATYE: *Patye scrub-bub-bub – Patye Dawes clean.*

DAWES: Patye, my dear girl. You are clean. You are so clean. And I
am not. *Dawes not clean. Not at all.*

Ah, my dear child. If you only knew what a filthy heart beat in this
chest. Look out there, beyond those heads. If you only knew the black
filth of the place we came from, how it marked all of us. All of us, me,
and Mr Johnson, and Mr Philip, all of us black and bringing a cargo
of blackness to this bright, clean place and to you. God forgive us.
You are clean. You are clean.

PATYE: *Missus scott Patye filthy black. Filthy black.*

DAWES: That does sound like her. She is wrong. You are black, but
lovely. When you can read better, I will read the Song of Songs to you.
Nigra es sed formosa. Formosa. Formosa. Beautiful. Your arms are so
thin. See, there's fairer skin beneath, here, where the sun doesn't get
to it. No, don't splash. You can't wash the rest of yourself to that!
Come here, come into the shade. Be black, be black and clean with
me.

Here, on the white sand. Look, how silver the gum is. It's clean, yes?

PATYE: *Yes, but Patye*

DAWES: See the fig, it's clean, yes? This soil—

PATYE: *Dust. Pemulgina*

DAWES: Yes, but clean, yes? No, don't stomp off.

PATYE: ...*taboa milijow!*

DAWES: Who's painted white? Me? Or you? Look, how can a shoulder like this be painted white? I am the whited sepulchre, not you. Everything in you is alive and clean, my beautiful girl. Come back to the tree. Yare badiow, kurigarang, miteeanga – ngalai yena?

Why are you laughing? Ah, my red skin – my back is burned by the sun. You see – you are not dirty. You are strong. You are stronger than the sun!

[*Patye gets up and leaves with her tub. The spotlight fades. We are back in the classroom.*]

You will excuse me children. I feel unwell. No. We will continue tomorrow. The same exercise, the fable.

FINIS

Crack'd

She left the web, she left the loom
She made three paces thro' the room
Alfred, Lord Tennyson, *The Lady of Shalott*

The mirror cracked from side to side. It had been a cheapie and was no great loss, but Elaine was having the kind of day in which a broken mirror was the last bloody straw.

She generally avoided looking out of the window. There was always something on the road beyond the river that she found annoying. Overworked horses, monocropping barley and rye, ignorant superstitious farmhands, and the inevitable riverbank lovers who rubbed salt in the wound of her singleness. She told herself that this was *her choice*, that she was taking a sabbatical from dating to focus on textile art, and that if her mother wanted to think that her only daughter was cursed to be a spinster, that was her problem.

Actually, the real problem was Lancelot, whose daily run along the river path was a torment to her hormones and her ears. Very few men could get away with leather, jewels, and a feathered hat. He sang out of tune, he peacocked, he needed a good haircut, and yet somehow his mighty silver bugle made up for all of it. Usually she managed to focus on the weaving, but a couple of times she'd slipped up and there had been a thing …. all very tiring and predictable, but you couldn't be thirty and find all your fun in weaving.

So with the mirror broken she threw down her shuttle and left the house. She got into the boat which had come with the place – 'four towers and positively *imbowered*,' the estate agent had said, omitting to mention the drawbacks of living on an island – and pushed off in the direction of Camelot in search of some fun in the form of Lancelot.

It was harder going than she had thought. There were deep shadows from the willow trees into which she kept getting snared. 'I am half sick of shadows,' she muttered through her teeth as she shoved off from the bank for the fourth time.

The boat also kept getting tangled in the gigantic lilies which Guinevere had stupidly seeded in the river, believing they would enhance Camelot's already hyper-romantic ambience. Exhausted with the struggle of steering around them, Elaine lay down in the boat. But even lilylocked, she could get no peace. The same moronic yokels who tormented her at home rambled past on the river path shouting questions and advice.

'You've got to go *with* the current, love!'

'Are you stuck, then?'

'D'you wanna hand there?'

'I'm fine!' she called back, wondering why they ignored her when she stood at the casement waving, but swarmed like flies now that she was stuck in a canoe. She took a deep breath and reminded herself that she was a strong, independent woman and that it was only a bloody boat.

Eventually, the lilies cleared, the river straightened, and the towers of Camelot approached. She lay down in the bottom of the boat and looked at the clouds. It was quite nice, lying there, drifting along on the current, humming to herself. After a bit she dozed off and was carried, sleeping, along the river into the city. It had been a rotten day. She was dead tired, and Camelot was quiet when she came floating in, so she only woke when a hefty male shadow blocked out the sun. She looked up to see Lancelot, who had been conducting a high-intensity interval class on the riverbank. He looked annoyingly attractive. She tried to look sleep-rumpled and winsome but her lips were dry from sleep-drool.

'She really does have a lovely face,' he was saying to a troop of glad damsels. 'God in his mercy send her grace.'

'Give me strength,' said the Lady of Shalott.

Hands

"There's power here," said Mr. Jaggers, *coolly tracing out the sinews with his forefinger. "Very few men have the power of wrist that this woman has."*
Charles Dickens, *Great Expectations*

Terrible people, they say, bring out the terrible parts in you. Jaggers was terrible. Not in the sense that he was a bad man, or any more immoral than a lawyer ever is, but terrible in the sense that God is: immense, remote, intractable. It is a mark of how terrible he was that I have never blamed him for the transformation which that night effected on me. I realized that it would be almost impossible for anyone to wield the kind of power Jaggers did over men's fates and perceptions and not to be altered by it.

I should also say that Jaggers' effect on the woman (and those men whom he saved from the Fleet, or the gallows, or Botany Bay) was beneficial, or at least better than the alternative. And of Providence's effect on Jaggers himself I can only speculate. I did not know him before – I doubt anyone did – so the transformation from simple youth to a man full of shadows and strange proclivities is the product of my own imagination. Not that I am known to be imaginative; my wife castigates me for my lack of imagination. No, all I can address with any integrity, of which Estella tells me I have precious little, is Jaggers' effect on me.

The genesis is easy enough to locate: the dinner, the only dinner, at his home in company with the tiresomely guileless Pirrip and the guilelessly tiresome Pocket. Why were they not transformed as I was? Because they were not prepared by life as I was. Like the parchment which is years in the preparation before the sharp quill incises the inky impress it will carry ever after, we three came to that gloomy place on Gerrard Street in different states of stretching, scraping, being made ready.

Jaggers saw in me some essential weakness which went beyond youthful boasting. It was the struggle with drink which dogs me still and the unwholesome sourness that causes a mutual dislike of the world and the fools in it. That part of him which was alert to weakness sniffed it out in me, seized it and, like a fisherman toying with something muscular and essentially stupid, reeled me in.

The woman was hardly in the room that night, but her fear, her dependence on his massy control, pervaded their half-empty house. Most of the rooms were unused, but Jaggers would have no lodgers, and liked the idea of the rooms above sitting in wait. Waiting for what, Pirrip asked, although I had already sensed that the answer involved waiting on his pleasure, a still, silent kingdom of rooms in which his will reigned.

If you thought of the woman as one more space made immanent with his wishes, she was a room more splendid than a mere housekeeper's closet. She was a ballroom, a royal audience hall, a temple of subjection, entirely oriented to him like a lodestone to an iron rod, a steeplechaser's mount to the crop-held hand. He was, in his way, an artist, a magician, in the delicacy with which he made the housekeeper twitch at his every move, unconnected by any wires which achieved this marionette act. Even as she set out the dishes, her eyes flickered to and from his mouth, his hands, the physical means of control and restraint which had seized her from the gallows and set about relentlessly, irresistible, shaping her world, her will, herself. I call that evening the beginning because I was aware of a double performance in this scene of domestic propriety. For Pirrip and Pocket Jaggers put on a flattering demonstration of adult regard by a professional man and his servant. For me, there was a calculated revelation of those drives which I had only just begun to recognize and from which I sought refuge in wine and arrogance.

Jaggers danced the conversation around to our prowess on the river. Callow and jostling, we rolled back our sleeves to show our forearms – as if true strength were vested in that assemblage of flesh and sinew! I saw the laugher in Jaggers' eyes, which dilated as he seized the woman's arm and bared it before us, heedless of her pleas.

The scars of absolute despair on one wrist, his intimation of the murderous strength in the other, her whispered urgency, the perfume of her abasement, the flesh-on-flesh assertion of his dominance – in which she was saved, not damned – it all merged into a moment of exquisite pain and tension in which the man I am now was born. I looked around blurrily at Pocket and Pirrip and saw an echo of my own fascination, mixed with a faint embarrassment.

A door to my boyhood, that time of confusion and dissatisfaction and distance, had slammed resoundingly shut. I was newborn, in a Soho house, with my newly-recognized needs and barren proclivities bared to the world like a babe. Jaggers' straight mouth twitched with a wholly internal laughter, and from somewhere deep within their complex and private game, I thought the woman laughed at me too.

Then he threw us out into the street, where the other two commenced a leisurely walk back to Pirrip's rooms. I remained in Gerrard Street, staring in disbelief at the house in which I fear I had been brought to the surface and left quite alone, without air.

I must go down to the seas again

I must go down to the seas again, for the call of the running tide
Is a wild call and a clear call that may not be denied
John Masefield

The first babies born with it were surgically corrected. It was a minor interdigital anomaly and not that unusual, said paediatric surgeons. We had once had fins, which became wings, then arms, and finally mammalian fingers, so the reappearance of webbing between the fingers was nothing new. In the smaller conferences and journals, surgeons surprised each other with the number of children showing such a reappearance, but no one made the connection between this atavism and the fact that nine-tenths of the affected babies were born in island nations quickly being submerged by the rising seas.

It was only when children began to be born in landlocked countries like Nepal, Kazakhstan, and Bolivia, with undeniable signs of some devolutionary process, of their cells feeling that they must go down to the sea again, that relevant agencies took it seriously. In a world reduced to one of two responses - civil disobedience or lipid apathy – no one knew quite how to respond to these new creatures (or rather, extremely old creatures, which had reinserted themselves into family trees like a bad driver coming up the hard shoulder, determined to push in). The children had functional lungs and could use their extremities as either hand or fin, so there was no immediate reason to panic.

Different nations responded differently. The Oceanic Federation, where most of the first children had been born, had realized that the children were functional on land but thrived in the water. Released into the ocean, they formed schools and shoals around the age of six, and then largely left their parents. With the fishing industry dead anyway, the OFe government banned fishing in its waters and mostly left the children to it. Persistent parents tried to track their children with solar-powered drones that buzzed about the insatiable Pacific like a cloud of flies, but the children did not like this. They would lure the drones to water level with the promise of a wave or kiss for landlubberish parents, before dismembering and drowning them.

The Chinerican Union responded commercially. Within months a range of products under the brand My Little Atavism was launched. The wealthy could feed, clothe, accessorize, track, and share the growth of their merkids. The poor equipped theirs with harpoons, and there were, predictably, a few mass-harpoonings. Religious figures who had railed against the idea of evolution now saw either vindication and divine judgment in babies made in a fish-god's image.

It was difficult to taxonomise the fish to which mankind was returning. Apart from the Chinerican children, whose aberrant violence was a product of culture (they had been exposed to violent television and the strange doctrine of the individual, which had overwhelmed their ichthyian brains) the new generation of human-fish were more admirable than their parents.

They were peaceful, community-minded, and as frugal in satisfying their limited needs as their human ancestors had been spendthrift. They made their own entertainment without resort to, or understanding of, the problems of speech, vicariousness, or electricity. It was difficult to tell whether they had the capacity for abstract thought; the children became increasingly private as they grew, until one morning a window, a front door, would be found open and the child gone, down to the sea which called them so ineluctably.

Biologists predicted an eventual diversity of species and subspecies. The chordata diversified into vertebrata and invertebrate, and vertebrata to jawless fishes, tetrapods, bony fishes and so on. So these children's offspring would eventually diversify into different species, like a remix of the evolutionary chart-topper, homo sapiens. Nobody mentioned what would happen when there inevitably came the equivalent of a shark.

The Fair Unknown

[Bram Stoker's Jonathan Harker tells us that] *In the moonlight opposite me were three young women, ladies by their dress and manner. I thought at the time that I must be dreaming when I saw them, they threw no shadow on the floor. They came close to me, and looked at me for some time, and then whispered together. Two were dark, and had high aquiline noses, like the Count, and great dark, piercing eyes, that seemed to be almost red when contrasted with the pale yellow moon. The other was fair, as fair as can be, with great masses of golden hair and eyes like pale sapphires. I seemed somehow to know her face, and to know it in connection with some dreamy fear, but I could not recollect at the moment how or where. All three had brilliant white teeth that shone like pearls against the ruby of their voluptuous lips. There was something about them that made me uneasy, some longing and at the same time some deadly fear. I felt in my heart a wicked, burning desire that they would kiss me with those red lips. It is not good to note this down, lest some day it should meet Mina's eyes and cause her pain, but it is the truth. They whispered together, and then they all three laughed, such a silvery, musical laugh, but as hard as though the sound never could have come through the softness of human lips. It was like the intolerable, tingling sweetness of waterglasses when played on by a cunning hand. The fair girl shook her head coquettishly, and the other two urged her on.* [Here Stoker's passage ends.]

There was a single moment of pain, such as you feel when the skin is punctured, discreetly and deliberately, with a point of exquisite sharpness. I felt a susurration of breath, but whether hers or mine I could not tell. In some diabolical way which subsumed the merely physical, we were as one body, one heart, one respiration. Then there was a terrible sensation of sucking, drawing out of me my very heart's blood.

With the last drop of strength and will that I possessed, I opened my eyes fully and put my hands on the fair woman's shoulders to push her away from me. She felt my resistance and looked up, the blood trickling, unswallowed, down her chin. Then it came to me, as those sapphire eyes fixed on mine beneath her dark lashes, where I had seen her before.

Some years ago, attending an elderly client who lived in the East End I had been importuned by one of the unfortunates who ply their trade in those evil-smelling streets. I will not mention the client's name, except to say that his family had long been resident in that area, having to do with the commerce of the docks, and had seen the notorious character of the place grow up around them. Descending from the cab before the client's house, she had caught my arm as I paid the driver and offered me what such unfortunate women do.

This was some years before I met Mina. I was young and unused to the nature of that quarter and the desolate, desperate souls who populate it. I flung her off, throwing her to the ground and knocking off her bonnet, which rolled into the stinking wet gutter. A fan of brilliant golden hair, like a spilled wheatsheaf, spread around her, and her blue eyes looked up into mine with hurt and confusion. I realised with horror that she was little more than a child, and stopped to offer my hand. She knocked it aside and sprang to her feet. 'Curse you!' she said, and it sounded dreadful from a child's mouth. 'For that knock, mister, I'll fetch you another, even if it takes a 'undred year! Just see if I don't!' and she turned, and fled down the dingy Whitechapel street.

Now, a world away, I realised she had made good on her oath. I, who could have offered her assistance, even salvation, had harmed further a woman who had already been so greatly injured by Fortune and the world. And here in the worst bastion of devils she was waiting, as she perhaps always had, to requite me.

Labour

Their freedom of expression was at first incomprehensible to her, though she had no difficulty in reconciling it with a lofty chastity which in the Creole woman seems to be inborn and unmistakable.

Kate Chopin, *The Awakening*

What if it is? My God, better that Alphonse should see it for himself than he be brought in and I forced to explain from childbed. Or worse, that this wretched nurse talks. She hasn't so far, but you can't tell with those people.

You can't tell with anyone. That's the whole point about this stupid misadventure. I can't even be sure about myself. I can tell myself, but I can't tell *about* myself. I'm raving. Pain, this is how pain deranges you. They say it's a woman's punishment for the sins of Eve. Mandelet says you don't have to put up with it anymore. They can use morphine and some other thing; you come around with only the vague memory of pain and, *voila*, a baby in your arms.

And only the nurse's word that it's yours.

I can't – I can't…I can't afford to be forgetful for even a second. I can imagine it – I come to and find myself put aside, abandoned, Alphonse staring at the tiny thing and *knowing*. Oh God, no. It's too much of a risk.

Did that wail come from me? Every time, I surprise myself. Under our frills, our knitting, under the perfume and starch, the spotless linen, there's an animal, and pain. Maybe the animal is pain, or an animal in pain, or…I'm raving again.

Why do I get myself into these ridiculous situations?

Because I'm an animal. The treacherous Eve, who breeds and feeds and lies and beguiles and—God, *where* is Mandelet? And what is that nurse *doing*? The smell of cologne water makes me ill. And Edna, poor, stupid, naïve Edna with her sensitivities and her daubing and

124

panting after Robert Lebrun. Come here, you silly little fool, and watch the anguish of one who thought herself mistress of love. Look at the sweat, dear – it's not pain, but fear, and *learn*. Husbands, like the sign that you're not expecting a child, are inconvenient, but they're regular and necessary and even the silliest woman can manage them. Cast a husband away and what do you have? The state I'm now in, but without anyone to pay the doctor, bring you flowers, build that delightful garden wall of respectability behind which you can do anything – with discretion. Edna lacks discretion. Her preposterous obsession with integrity, honesty – as if these things were necessary for a marriage. Let her look. Let her wake up to herself.

Ah, God, it comes! I have only moments left of this, the whole world I have built. Alphonse is still not here; if he misses it – if it *is*, and *chère Saint Agnes*, let it not be – *quelle cauchemar!* If he misses it, the Griffe could take it away and get rid of it…No, no, that would be adding more sin to the pile. We must expect to pay for our actions at some point.

Why did I assure him my family was French through and through? Stupid, stupid girl! All that vain confidence in fidelity, all your belief at nineteen that a husband will be enough, more than enough – will be everything. Nothing, no one, is ever enough when the fire is in your blood. Ah…Mandelet! And *aaaah!!*

My God, give me my ... give it to me now!! Is it? Is it? Open your eyes, my angel! My ruddy little….ah! Thank God!

It is not. It's not. Not. Not. I am safe! We are safe! My child, my beautiful child. Alphonse's child. Come, my tiny angel, sleep on my breast and I will lay down a road of promises to heaven that I will never again betray my husband with a black man.

Toy Shop

"Take our love to Father!" cried Bobbie. And the others, too, shouted:—
"Take our love to Father!"
        E.Nesbit, *The Railway Children*

2nd December, 1903

Horse Guards lay white as a shirtfront under yesterday's snowfall. I reached Admiralty Arch in a shoeleathery squelch of meltwater. I imagined Batchelder staring balefully at my schoolboy antics from his window. He is – the Service is – immune to fanciful ideas like the first footprint in a snowy world. The Service's task, he reminded us, is of a great maintenance, a resolute holding back of governments' – *all* governments' – innovative impulses. Batchelder wears galoshes and rubber boots when it snows.

Lily suggested books for Bobbie; I was halfway up Charing Cross Road when I caught a glow in Cecil Court which had drawn half a dozen other wing-collared escapees. It turned out to be a toyshop – *magazina igrushek glinskaya* (*igrushek* was not in the Service Russian exam, though it should have been – it is 'child's toy'). Some clever engineer of children's delights had transformed the shop's single window into a birch-forest clearing. The trees, slim and silvery crowded together and a thick snow of powdered sugar covered their roots. Between the trunks the same engineer had contrived golden wolves' eyes from tiny lanterns and paper, blinking now here, now there. In the centre stood a wooden house from the legends of the taiga, its lace-curtained windows alive with firelight and the shadows of balalaika-players. It twirled, the little log house, on a single chicken leg, like a rebus from a medieval coat of arms.

We stood, clerks and office boys, myself, and two silks *en route* to a good dinner at Savage's or the Carlton, impearled by the glow of childhood. Then the door of the little house flew open and out upon a mechanical arm shot a terrifying crone, wielding a hatchet at her sodden-footed audience. Batchelder's low opinion of me would have been justified if he had seen how high I jumped. We gave each other sheepish grins and dispersed into the darkness of Covent Garden and Charing Cross Road.

A dark-haired young woman behind the counter welcomed me; she had a rich, pleasant contralto voice and the globular vowels of the French-speaking Russian. She wore a dress the colour of the darkest plum – I can't quite name the colour, but it struck me that I had never seen it in silk before. Clever, slightly sardonic dark eyes and a gaze that Englishwomen do not use. I complimented her window display. 'You must be the only person in London who can frighten a pair of barristers.'

She laughed frankly (how charming is frankness in a woman!) and bowed. 'You know the story of Baba Yaga?' she said. She had a habit of lifting an eyebrow as she speaks. The asymmetry was attractive – is this what the French call *jolie-laide*? – quizzical, comical, as knowing as a woman selling toys must be. I said, 'I have the tale in a small book of children's stories; I brought it from Russia last year for my children.'

She looked surprised. 'You have been to Russia?'

'For my work only, unfortunately. But your country is very beautiful, when the weather makes it possible to open one's eyes.' She bowed again slightly to this, smiling. I heard Batchelder's voice – grave, gloomy – *anyone, anywhere, at any time. You will not know what they are until they have a net around you and the secrets entrusted to you. Ultimate discretion, even from your very closest friends. Perhaps most of all, from your closest friends.*

'I have not been there for some time. My toys are sent to me here by a trusted cousin, but I prefer to remember it as I last saw it. In the summer, with the sun shining on the Neva and very few soldiers on the streets.'

I understood the reference. When I had last been there, Sipyagin, the Interior minister and head of their bestial spiderweb of secret police, had been assassinated. The repercussions were as noisy and messy as Russian public affairs always seem to be. Tired of the shouting beneath my hotel windows, I returned to England. Batchelder had been unimpressed by my lack of stamina; he had hopes that I would catch wind of something. When I enquired about *what* exactly, he had been vague. I was removed from the Russia office and sent, like a disappointing gun dog, next door to Japan.

She smiled again. 'But toys have only the history that we give them, which makes them much better playthings than politics, I think.'

I laughed outright at that. We caught each other's eyes; I have a notion that we saw something of each other. I'm probably wrong. Believing you see yourself in someone else is usually the first step in an embarrassment. 'What can I show you?' she asked.

I described Bobbie; she showed some beautiful books of fairytales. For Phyllis I took a child's samovar and glasses, a sugar bowl and tongs, painted with branches which seemed to burst into flames of blue flowers. A comical bear, in glistening varnished wood, split logs with a mechanical hatchet, a weary look on his face, the cogs within his belly grumbling like hunger – I imagined Peter enjoying it.

A doll in the cabinet caught my eye; she brought it out and placed it on the counter, silently watching me. She is a clever woman, I think, and it is pleasant to meet clever women before we lose them to children and that strange domestic country for which I have no letter of introduction, no diplomatic papers, only the immunity of being a breadwinner.

It was a large wooden doll shaped like a skittle, with the face of a sweet babushka under a painted headscarf of lace. A line ran around the middle. We smiled at each other; I felt that Madam Glinskaya was testing me with this toy, somehow, and it was my pleasure to be tested.

'A daruma doll? But these are Japanese.' Her glance shot to the side ever so slightly.

'You know Japan as well?'

'I was there … recently.'

'Also for your work? What can I show this well-travelled man that will surprise him?'

She twisted the shiny head and body apart. Within there was another doll, the same shape, but smaller. A prince, clad in a blue tunic with white lace, a small sword painted on his belt. I took the prince from her hands and opened him. Within was his horse, within that, a wolf. Within the wolf was a king, grey and grim and clearly wicked. Then a second horse, white of coat with a golden mane, and within him a second wicked king. Within the king was a princess. Within the princess was a golden cage, and within the cage was a bird, the smallest of the dolls, of fantastic plumage, golden and flaming. The firebird.

Madam Glinskaya lined them along the counter as I opened each doll, laughing at my eagerness to get within the mystery. Ten dolls in all, each within the other. 'They are called matryoshka,' she said. 'Mother-dolls. This one tells the story of Prince Ivan, Grey Wolf, and the Firebird.'

Each office in our warren should have a matryoshka; we could shelve it between the Foreign Office List and Wisden. If I were Batchelder, I should give one to the new boys, along with his usual speech. *This will be your task – disjoining one layer of a story from another, considering – as far as you are permitted – whether the lie within was the parent or child of the lie which encased it. Multiple fictions which lurk within each other, inaccessible unless you unscrew them in the correct sequence. Play with this doll and you will know the Great Game.* Japan, Russia, Britain, the tangle of alliances and lies which prevents empires from swallowing each other like monstrous dolls. Could you still bear to make this your life's work?

The woman saw me take in her toys. They always mean something else, darker and infinitely sadder to the parent who buys them for the child.

'You understand, I think, what these mean for us. Something different than for your children,' she said softly. The fire snapped in the grate and I felt myself lose myself, somehow. 'Bring your children and I will tell them the story of a prince and his friend, the Gray Wolf.'

I will bring the children to the *magazina igrushek*. I have a notion to hear this story, told by a Russian. I took the matryoshka for myself. I will have it on the mantlepiece in my study, and I shall keep my heart in the innermost one, so that I do not take it abroad or into Batchelder's snares. I have found the entrance to the wild woods in Cecil Court, but I cannot tell if the woman is the princess or the wolf.

Superposition

It is typical of these cases that an indeterminacy originally restricted to the atomic domain becomes transformed into macroscopic indeterminacy, which can then be resolved by direct observation. That prevents us from so naïvely accepting as valid a "blurred model" for representing reality. In itself, it would not embody anything unclear or contradictory. There is a difference between a shaky or out-of-focus photograph and a snapshot of clouds and fog banks.
Erwin Schrödinger, 'The present situation in quantum mechanics'

A fog rises from the river, creeping over Christchurch meadow and Merton Street. Soon it will invade the Magdalen cloister and twist up the stairwells, settling in the library vestibule. He watches it from the apartment on Rose Street which they have given him. He knows that the fog will not be permitted into the library. Nothing indefinite is, except the fellows. He also knows that his apartment is referred to as Babylon, because of his equally indefinite family arrangements. Like the fog in the library, you are either in or out. Nothing unimportant is left unresolved in Oxford. Only the larger questions are encouraged to linger, like a running sore, to become someone's life work.

He sighs and turns away from the window. It has been an exhausting day. His wife has wept for most of it, over a cat which had begun to frequent their house, and which was seen dead on the High, a tumble of matted fur, barely feline after repeated runnings-over from vehicle wheels. His mistress, who is expecting their child, was told about the cat at lunch (by his wife) and added her own tears. A colleague's small daughter, who is staying with them, heard about the cat at dinner and wept copiously through pudding.

He can see why the Senior Common Room calls his home Babylon.

Now both women are reading to the child in the bedroom, from which he has been banished for the duration of the child's stay. His wife, his mistress, and their six-year-old charge all sleeping in the largest bed which Magdalen College owns, while he, who has just won the Nobel Prize, sleeps on the sofa. So goes the wave function, he thinks, wondering whether the sofa is wide enough to turn over on. He wonders which bit of the whole experiment will cause the wave of tolerance, which he has ridden from Breslau to Zurich, to Berlin and now Oxford, to collapse.

Next door their voices, low and soothing, remind him of the female realm from which he is shut out for the night. He listens more closely. Together they are telling the child another hausmarch from Grimm. The little girl has been delighted to discover that the German versions – originals, he thinks, some things *are* definite – of her English bedside tales are infinitely bloodier, more perverse and impossible to predict. There is rarely a happy ending. The child has taught them that 'happily ever after' is almost obligatory in English children's tales. They have taught her that *glücklich bis ans Lebensende* is not, in German ones.

Surely, he thinks, the point is that you cannot know. You must read to the end to find out whether the wicked queen simply fades away or dances to her death in a pair of red-hot iron shoes. Or whether the boy murdered by his stepmother becomes a bird, or a murderer in turn.

They are telling her *Die drei Schlangenblätter*. A princess agrees to marry anyone who is prepared to be buried alive with her, if she should die before them. Repelled by the conditions, her peers refuse. Only a poor woodsman agrees.

The child is asking questions. 'What is the man dies first? Will she be buried with him?'

Anny, his wife. 'No. She'll just keep living.'

The child is indignant. 'That's not fair!'

Hilde, his mistress. The wife of his laboratory assistant, who is himself sleeping with Anny. The whole thing is like a lemniscate. 'It's not fair, but that's what they agreed. It doesn't have to be fair, if you agree to it.'

Behind the door, he imagines the women smiling at each other.

'So does she die first?'

'She does. And down into the vaults, into the cold crypt of the church, they put her body. And they shut him in with it, just him and his dead wife and a single candle in an ocean of musty dark space. Sealed in, so he can't get out.'

He imagines the child's eyes, huge above the college-issue bedsheets. 'What happens?' It is a mere whisper. Her parents would be furious to know they were filling the child full of these stories. The English, in their dark, damp little island, hemmed in by river mists and their suspicion of foreignness, detest the morbid even as they embody it. They practice a jollity which is by turns ridiculous and awesome. But it precludes acceptance of him and his unorthodox household, regardless of the Nobel.

'Who knows what happens in a sealed tomb?' Hilde again.

'Maybe she's not dead,' the child says hopefully.

'Oh, she's dead alright,' Anny says.

'But how do you know, if the tomb's sealed?' The child's persistence, her ability to put her finger on the pertinent question, astonishes him. Almost as much as how bright her voice is, when a mere hour before she had been sobbing so hard over a dead cat that she could barely speak.

'We know, because we're telling the story.'

'So you know what happens?'

'Mostly. Unless the story changes its mind halfway through,' says Anny.

'It does that sometimes,' Hilde adds. 'And you just have to follow along, not knowing.'

'So he sits there in the dark, and just as his candle's about to go out, what do you think he sees in the corner of the crypt?'

'An angel?' the child says.

'No. Try again.'

'A demon?'

'It's not always one or the other. What's the last thing you'd want to see, alone in a crypt with your dead wife?'

'The college president,' the child says, promptly. 'He smells like aniseed balls.' There is laugher on both sides of the door.

'A snake.'

'Truly?'

'Truly. So he jumps up and hacks it in three pieces.'

'Poor snake,' the child says, reprovingly. 'That's not kind.'

No, he thinks, it is not kind. He wills her to ask the better question, about whence came the snake, and if the man knows that, why he can't go thence. But she does not ask, and he loses interest and returns to the window to look at the fog, and think about agreements which lead to tombs.

He has a letter to write to Copenhagen. It lies unfinished on his desk, but he cannot withdraw from the window and the coiling soft whiteness which decoheres this riverbound town from time and space.

Princes in tombs and the storyteller in their superposition above it all, and children in beds that are mere islands in the river of possibilities, and men watching the fog which may be watching him, and the impossibility of the mind believing that each moment is only one of many co-continuous billions of moments. And within the next room, within the body of his mistress grows another nexus of possibilities, locked in its own steel box of life. It can be told, but not understood.

Schrödinger crosses the room and gently opens the door. On the bed, in positions of rest, are the women and the child, and deep in the nest of sheets and women's stories, sleeps the cat.

Journey of A Mage

...were we led all that way for
Birth or death?
T.S. Eliot, 'Journey of the Magi'

Set down this, he said, *set down this*. And I did, although I was not there as a scribe. I set down his story about following a star in his youth, and how it led him to the land of my own people, where he found only cold, winter hills, a poor bare town and a hundred thousand of us Jews scurrying around for the census. I took down as best I could his ramblings about shepherds and lambs, a poor young couple with an early baby and – though I did not understand it – the feeling of dread that came over him when he saw this child, and which he said had followed him since.

Unusually for me, Ephraim Ben Sirach, who am known as a purveyor of the choicest, the rarest objects, to kings and even the Caesars, and whose chieftest delight is to make a profit from those who turned my people into slaves – unusually for me, I pitied the magus.

I could afford to pity him. He had bought my entire load: Indian ivories, lapis from Bamiyan, the strange celadon pots which ring like a bell and are made in secret places in the great kingdom beyond the wall. When I mentioned that I was born in the same year he described, the year of Caesar Augustus' census, he gripped my arm and asked me what I knew about the star that had shone during that winter, and which had, for his fellow astronomers, presaged some conjunction between heaven and earth. They thought of it as a bridge over which they expected who-knew-what or whom to come walking.

I smiled, I remember, and tried to move the talk along. I am tired of seeing my people thought of as lunatics, hysterics, weaklings under the boot of Rome. 'Just legends, my lord. The stories of all captive people who hope for a messiah to break their shackles because they cannot break them for themselves.'

'Messiah – this is what we call a saoshyant.' He looked into the distance.

'Who will arrive on a bridge of stars
Bringing with him the sword of Ahura Mazda
Banishing the Druj, renewing the world
By the fire of virtue.'

I nodded. I had no idea what he was talking about, but I heard bitterness behind the words. I am a merchant, but even I know that a man must believe in something, and that he is as one widowed when that faith dies away. 'Certainly, there was one born in that year, near the town you describe, of whose birth stories are told.' I didn't say *unlikely* stories, or *ridiculous*.

Again came the iron grip on my arm. 'Tell me.'

I wanted to say, 'Set down this. Set down this,' and treat him like a scribe. Instead I told him about the old couple who had had no children and of the son suddenly born to them after an angel visited the woman, Elisheba, when her husband was in the Temple. I told him about how they named the child Yokhanan and how he took himself off to the wilderness, living on locusts and honey and wearing a tunic of camel hair. He claimed that the spirit of the Lord visited him during the nights among the stones and stars and commanded him to go back to the towns and begin washing people of their sins.

The man watched me with the gaze of a lion watching a gazelle. He did not withdraw that vice-like gaze even when I told him that Yokhanan's insistence on sin eventually tired even Herod Antipas, that Greek puppet the Romans have made our king. Or that Herod had him beheaded one evening as a gift for Salome, his stepchild.

He asked only one question. 'The man had followers, surely, who continue his work of sin-washing?'

I conceded that this was true, though I held back the fact that Judea is now full of such characters, some of whom claim to fly, or command storms, and even to have conquered death. I also omitted my relationship to Yokhanan, who is my cousin, and that lunacy runs in my mother's family.

He released me, and it seems that I released him in some way. I heard that he had regained a vigour lost for more than forty years, and that he set out for Judea shortly after I left. He died in the fertile land near the Euphrates from age and some fever, but his servants, whom I met in a caravanserai near Damascus, said that he died happy, even transformed.

Death's Dream Kingdom

Shape without form, shade without colour,
Paralysed force, gesture without motion
T.S. Eliot, 'The Hollow Men'

I acquire new forms on average every 0.6 seconds. I rarely take a rest, but when I do, I have always basked in the stasis of a single form, to be precise. I don't do much when I'm like this. I wander around shops, drink with that body's friends, sleep (a confusing experience for me, and not one I'm that fond of, since it's too much like a busman's holiday). Once I had a baby. I cut that break short and returned to work unexpectedly; the dissolution of my (appropriated) self in the suckling baby was too difficult, too reminiscent of something... though I don't know what. After all, how can Death remember a mother? Or, conversely, be one? So I went back to my round of dissolving into people, or dissolving them into me, whichever is easier to imagine, and changing their position in that dream kingdom which is always and everywhere.

It probably sounds back-to-front to you. You have a body and a soul (or mind, or chi, or anima, depending on your preference of verbal sign). They separate when the heart stops squeezing and the last breath rattles out of the lungs, like the last shopper in a department store being escorted out at closing time. The body goes into a box, with or without a quick flame-grilling, and the soul goes to a place that cartographers haven't got round to locating. You continue to exist, so you believe, in memory.

In fact, it's nothing like that at all.

You are all part of me. You circle me like electrons whizzing around a nucleus. Eventually you fall into me and the atomic number of the whole shifts, infinitesimally. But there was never a time when you were not part of me. What you call your life, and the

138

unremembered time before that, and the unrememberable time after it, is all part of this dream kingdom. That is the nature of dreams: you can't be sure whether you're awake or asleep, alive or dead. Whether you're you or me.

That's why it's preposterous to fear me. You are me. You lose nothing and go nowhere. Your heart stops and, like the lights going on in your darkened living room and friends jumping out shouting 'Surprise!', you realize the real nature of a situation in which you have been immersed all along.

Your last breath passes through your lips and you shake yourself and think, *Sleep, prepare for life*. Your life has been death's dream kingdom and you are the thing you have feared most.

The Last Twist of the Knife

Here is what we cannot say: life is an imposition upon those who do not yet exist and who, by being born, are thrust into a dreadful world of exhaustion and ceaseless, vicious self-awareness.

Do you have children? Then you have done more than put riders on the carousel of suffering. You have sculpted the horses, skewered them with the carousel poles, wound up the tinny music that hides the screams. You have built the lie, gilded it, and drafted in more victims.

Now imagine being told this in a classroom full of teenagers whom you're leading through Eliot's poetry. Fifty eyes on you, wanting to see you justify it all. Of course you'll punish the accuser. Of course you'll say this misery is subjective. Of course you'll back down from your platform and tell them it's only a poem and oh look, the bell's about to go. They'll file out and you'll wonder – what the hell just happened?

It started with a discussion about insomnia and Eliot's 'Rhapsody on a Windy Night.' Animals don't suffer insomnia. Only people combine the physical discomfort of sleeplessness with our big brain's awareness of what happens when we can't sleep. Only we can project forward and fear the sleepless future, the madness attendant on insomnia.

And clearly, you said, the persona in Eliot's 'Rhapsody' is already showing signs of that madness. Talking streetlamps, dribs and drabs of French, the obsession with time. The tortures of the human memory, which is an incredible thing until the mind malfunctions.

And then what? A night-time world full of grotesqueries, 'the madman shaking a dead geranium', things strange in themselves and made stranger by incorporation into the exhausting logic of the persona's insomnia-addled brain. The crowd of twisted things.

It's the modern condition, says one student, upon whom you turn the smile of a teacher who recognizes their own words. It's the result of a world too crammed with new inventions, and the punishing demands of the world of work. It's the isolation of the tiny human consciousness in an unnatural state – the state of the city. It's alienation.

Yes, yes, and yes, you nod, feeling vindicated that your own interpretation of Eliot's poetry, carefully pushed into the gaping beaks of these little chicks who will regurgitate it in carefully-organized body paragraphs, has been so thoroughly digested. You say, This is the poetic fantasia which shows us what life is really like, under the skin, on the flip side of the waking world, in the private moments where you allow yourself to sag under the massive lie of it all. It's like Banksy, turning his trademark existential misery up[on a Singin' in the Rain streetscape, showing how life wears down and warps one tiny consciousness.

You're pretty chuffed. You anticipate some good essays at the end of the year. This bunch really gets it.

So why, the kid goes on.

Why what, you beam.

Why have kids, if this is what life's like?

Well, you say, thinking of your own well-adjusted brood. Well, it's not like that for everybody. Eliot lived at a difficult time in history. He had trouble with relationships. Look at 'Prufrock.'

In 'Prufrock', says the kid, at least Eliot seems able to laugh at himself and all the other epiphany-pushing wanker Modernists. This, 'Rhapsody', this is like mental illness. Hallucinating, sleepless, cut off, hyper-awake. But still required to keep his end up. Shine his shoes, account for himself. Pay his way. Fit in and contribute.

You feel faintly uneasy and wonder where it's all going. How could this be refocused for an exam essay? Maybe, you say, maybe the

141

persona is a kind of caricature of things we think and do, but it's concentrated into one poem.

You say, with more conviction than you feel, Life isn't really *that* exhausting, *that* grotesque.

But it is, the kid persists. I'm often sleepless. The world usually seems at least this weird to me. And when you come across someone else who's experienced it it's a relief. What bothers me is how we read this together, agree that life can really *suck* for at least one person – who's not even that unusual – just because of the ordinary stuff; work, girls, sleeplessness, ugly surroundings. And then we just park this in some classroom. We're supposed to be learning for life, but throughout the school day we're told the opposite of this poem – mostly by people who look exhausted. Or we're told how to manage The Suck. Nobody addresses the obvious truth: that if this is what life is like, or even *can* be like, then you have no right to give it to someone else.

Well you don't have to, you tell him. You can go and live your life any way you want.

But I'm interested in you, he says. You obviously agree on the interpretation: life really can be this terrible. What would you do if *your* kid was the one wandering about at night, listening to talking streetlamps, thinking the moon wore face powder, going to bed every night knowing that he has to wake up and face the lie the next day?

This isn't about me, you say stiffly.

Yes it is, he says. It's about you and everyone else who gets all rhetorical when you're interpreting stuff and exhorting us to develop our own meanings, and then does the exact opposite to what you've just said. It's about not acting consistently with what you put over as some kind of philosophical truth. Remember, it only needs one case to make it valid – if even *one* person has a life like the persona in 'Rhapsody' – or 'The Hollow Men' or the Magi, or any of the poems – then how can you possibly justify the risk of bringing a kid into a life like that?

142

Is there a point to all this, you say wearily, wishing for a staffroom coffee, which seems less bitter than this kid. Or do you just want to call me a hypocrite?

Just that life's not worth it, he says without a smile. If there's even one person who wound up enduring nights like this, that should be enough to stop everyone from having kids. It should plug that running tap of pop psychology and pep that we get in assembly.

Speaking of which, you say gratefully ...the bell.

And they leave, and you leave, and the classroom sits empty, until you see them tomorrow and are confronted again by students who want you to be consistent with the meaning you see in the poetry.

The last twist of the knife.

Ergasterion

Ullmann had suffered badly from motion sickness on the way, so badly that he had taken pills for it. He swallowed them and lay down on the seat, breathing deeply and trying to ignore the awful rocking. He watched the birch treetops speed past, many millions of them, for hour after hour, until the nausea passed. Just once he was gripped by an impulse to tell the driver to stop, and to get out and breathe the cold sharp air of the taiga. But he did not, because he knew that the car would not stop until they had reached the quarry, or one of them died.

He must have slept, he thought, because when he woke they had stopped, but he had no memory of why he was there, or even who he was.

The driver announced their arrival by sounding the horn before the great wooden gates. A man in a grey tunic in the Russian style dragged the gates open, the barbed wire along the top swaying with the movement. He saluted as they rolled through; Ullmann noticed the grey tinge to his skin and the shadows beneath his cheekbones.

There was a short driveway and a scrubby oval of grass in front of a two-storey building of pale brick with tall, pleasant windows. The building's general design looked as if it had begun as a villa before being turned into an administration building. Three wide steps led to a set of double front doors, which were open and through which more men and women in grey tunics were coming. Behind the administration building he could see many rows of rough birchwood long huts, with shingled roofs and a chimney at each end.

He tried to sit up straight and look official. He was still torn between considerable confusion about who he was and the purpose of his visit, and a desire to be pleasant and agreeable. Briefly, he considered explaining that the journey had disoriented him and that he would retire for the night but be entirely at their disposal in the morning. Just as quickly he dismissed the idea. He had a feeling – although whence he could not say – that he was expected to *try*, and that anything less, including an honest plea of sickness and confusion, would make him look less, and this would not do.

Less than what? he thought, as the driver parked the car before a large grey villa. A portly man with a moustache like Stalin's, wearing an outfit which was neither a uniform nor a dress suit, stepped forward and shook Ullmann's hand. *If I'm not sure what I'm doing here, how can I be worried about being more or less?* He smiled at the foolishness of it. Noticing his smile, the reception party seemed to relax slightly and smile as well. It crossed his mind that it would be comical if they were as confused as he was. Everyone's smile increased.

The building sat on a kind of escarpment, with the huge half-moon of the quarry behind it. A reception had been laid on in a large room with a vast window from which they could see everything that was happening in the quarry and the huts below. A short speech of welcome was made by the man with the Stalin-moustache, from which Ullmann deduced that he, Ullmann, was there to inspect the operations, to make sure the workers were fairly treated, and to contribute recommendations for improvement. They were, the man said, always keen to improve.

Ullmann listened gratefully, shook some hands, and then turned to the window, which ran the length of the room. The vast grey bowl of the quarry and all the work gangs which laboured in and around it were presented like a film. The moustached man was stood at his side. 'How long has the quarry been worked?' Ullmann asked.

A look of surprise crossed the man's face, as if the question had never occurred to him and said, 'I've no idea. It must have started at the surface and been worked inward, if that gives you any idea. Given how deep it goes, a long time. I've always thought of it as being as old as the world.' He gave a short laugh.

'And always a colony like this?'

The man gestured to the dust, the invariant gray which clothed people and rocks, sky and machinery. 'Who else would come to this place?'

Ulmann made a careful scan of the scene, beginning at one end of the granite bowl. The workers' huts were divided between the two arms of the half-moon, with the quarry between them. The man explained that families were in the huts nearest the main building, single workers in those further away. Ullmann turned in surprise. 'I wasn't aware that we had entire families here.'

'They don't arrive that way,' the man said, 'but sooner or later most workers conspire to meet, then we have the problem of expectant mothers. Besides, it's much easier to move them all in together and let them form families, in a civilized manner, as it were.'

'You don't mean to say that children are born here?' Ullmann said in horror.

'Of course!' the man replied. 'How else would the quarry continue to be mined?' He gave a great laugh and put a hand under Ullmann's arm, moving him along the scene a little. It was impossible to tell whether he was joking or not.

At the farthest part of the quarry, several tiers down, a work gang made tiny by the distance laboured at the rock. Some men were hacking at it with picks, others loading the fallen rocks into barrows and wheeling them to the gigantic rockfall which joined the two arms of the half-moon. When they could go no further along the road – which was easily wide enough to have taken a bulldozer – they tipped the barrows off the edge, adding to the tumble of the rocks. 'Won't that just fill the quarry in eventually?' said Ullmann, watching a single ant-sized figure right his empty barrow and begin the long walk to where his workmates waited to refill it.

'Not in the lifetime of anyone here,' said the man.

'But what's the point of it?' Ullmann asked, puzzled.

The man's forehead creased a little. 'Well, I suppose if you look at it *that* way, there's none,' he said. 'But focus on the effect of the work on the individual and it's immense. Everything you see gives these people something to do, without which there's only the agony of time – time spent with yourself— and who wants that!' He laughed uproariously. 'No, but seriously; you must focus on how the work empowers the individual, makes them aware of their agency – though not too aware, obviously. It gives them a passion for creating something, even if it's pointless to other people, something that shows the basic process of cause and effect. Such a focus offers you a whole new perspective. A much more positive one, too,' he finished reprovingly.

'That seems like a bit of an illusion,' said Ullmann. 'If they don't particularly enjoy hacking out the rock and then filling it in again, their sense of empowerment will surely feel a bit fraudulent, to say the least.'

'It's all in the mind,' the man said. 'Perspective – choice of perspective – is everything. But you're right to take that stance; it's valuable.' He took Ullmann's elbow again and peered at him seriously. 'This is why we welcome new eyes – it's so valuable to have a new view of what we do, it really is. You must feel free to make these valuable observations while you're here.' He squeezed the elbow and let it go.

A woman appeared at Ullmann's side, holding a tray of drinks. She wore the same grey uniform as the others, with brown hair swept severely to one side and tied beneath one ear. Although neither beautiful nor ugly, she had an intensely alive face. Surprised by her sudden appearance at his elbow, Ullmann smiled. She looked directly into his eyes and he had the sense that she knew exactly how confused he was about being in the place. She handed him a glass and turned away. He watched her moving through the room until he became aware that the others were watching him with something like approval as he gazed at her. He cleared his throat and turned back to the window, but before his mind's eye he still saw her extraordinary face and quizzical half-smile.

The sun had dropped to the edge of the quarry rim. Lights were turned on in the reception room; he thought about how the place must look to the workers returning to their huts; the warm rectangles of light, the silhouettes of people moving freely among the wine and crystal. But the window was so large that the darkness outside seemed to Ullman to overshadow the room and take the warmth out of the light. He felt suddenly weary and desperate to be alone and curled into himself.

He intimated to the moustached man that he had felt unwell on the journey and would be glad of an early night – the better to get down to work in the morning, he said hastily. The man looked curiously at him. 'Are you sure?' he said.

'Quite sure,' Ullmann said. 'I'm afraid. If you'll forgive me.'

He felt a kind of lull of surprise in the others in the room, but he was beginning to tire of the whole thing and of his own confusion, and so ignored it. 'Well,' said the man, finishing his drink and setting the empty glass down, 'well then. Let me show you to your quarters.' Ullmann made a general bow in the direction of the room and they left.

He was led to a small hut, almost a garden shed, between the administration building and the family huts. There was a single square window and a flimsy-looking door. The place would be freezing in the winter. He tried not to show his surprise and dismay at these miserable quarters. It was only for one night, he told himself, and besides, he was desperate to be alone. The journey, the effort of being pleasant and concealing his strange amnesia about his purpose there, had made him ragged and fretful and now he wanted nothing so much as to lie down and lose himself in sleep.

The man threw open the door with a lordly air and wished him a sound sleep. 'Tomorrow,' he said, 'the work begins!' He saluted Ullmann and departed towards the family huts.

Without waiting for him to disappear fully from sight, Ullmann shut the door. There was a single bed made up with a white pillow and rough gray blanket stamped with the colony's name, a chair, table, and washstand. He lay down on the bed without taking his shoes off, and was asleep instantly.

He woke to the feeling of a cool hand moving across his bared chest. Before he was even fully awake he knew that it was the woman from the reception. She sat on his bed in the moonlight, bare breasted as a statue, a worker's overcoat around her waist and legs, smiling down at him. Behind her the full moon shone a pale nimbus around her head, and a field of blue radiance fell on her shoulders.

'How did you get in?'

'It wasn't locked.'

'I meant how did you get out of your own—' He didn't know what to say, since *hut* sounded demeaning.

'That's not really locked either,' she said.

'Not locked?'

There was no point in asking her name. 'Have you been sent?' he said, looking up at her.

'Why would I have been sent?'

'Perhaps to test me. To compromise what I'm here to do.'

She laughed. 'And what is that?'

'To inspect the place and make suggestions. To write some kind of report about standards.'

She put her hand on his chest again and leaned towards his face. 'You don't sound sure of what you're doing here,' she whispered.

He was awash with confusion and sensation and began several sentences about why he could not do with her what she was in the very process of doing. But he was so engaged in trying to sort out these ideas that the thing he could not do had happened and was over

149

and she was sinking onto his chest before he had reached any conclusion.

He lay still; she curled around herself beside him like a whelk in a fingernail of water and he held her as their hearts slowed. He lifted her hand in his and looked at it in the white light pouring from the window. It was without dust or callouses or any sign that she had laboured in the quarry. 'What do you do here?'

'I do this,' she said simply, without moving her head from his chest.

He struggled to sit up. 'You don't mean *this* is your task here?' he said. A sense of nausea came over him again, a kind of hot disorientation like the feeling he had had in the car.

She shrugged. 'Handing around wine glasses isn't a necessary task,' she said wryly.

Ullmann began to say something about it being monstrous that she had been pressed into selling herself, but she stopped his mouth with a kiss. 'I wasn't pressed into it,' she said. 'No one has ever even spoken of it to me, much less said in so many words that this is what I would do here. In fact, I realized some time ago that I could have left. I stay because I can't think of anywhere else to go, which makes one place as good as another.'

'But you're here with so many…' He was again lost for a name that was neither insulting or horrifying.

'So many just like me,' she finished. 'At least I can pity the others, even if I revolt myself by what I do to them in order to survive.'

'Do to them?' said Ullmann. 'What do you do?'

'Why this, of course,' she said.

'But how is this revolting?'

She sighed. 'As you said, any of us could leave at any time, but we choose to stay, partly from a fear of freedom and because, once you know this place and have a handful of names to hold onto it is bearable, even if it is rarely more than that. I stay because I am afraid to go, and because at times I perform my job well – even if it is a hateful one. My only task is to do this: not to sell myself to those who have just come here, although that is often part of it. No, it's to give them a reason to stay, to make them believe that some need or desire can be answered through another person here. And with that desire fulfilled – although it is never fully assuaged – it gladdens the whole place and gives it the illusion of somewhere one could be happy. Sometimes I perform my job so well that we both forget for a time that there is anything outside this place. But then, for me at least, something always causes it to pall, and I begin to remember again that I am only doing a job and an illusory one at that. And then I cannot bear myself, or this place which I serve by entrapping people to stay.'

'But you are in exactly the same position as those you entrap. How do you know that they are not charged with the same task, and are out to entrap you?'

'But they are,' she said softly, 'and that's the dreadful pity of it. They entrap and want to be trapped; then they want freedom and are afraid to be free. And it is all endless. It simply never stops.'

'Can you not make up your mind to being here, then, and be happy about it, if you're all in the same situation, and all equally guilty of snaring each other?'

'Living together brings out the horrors of our own nature. It makes it impossible to be happy. You could build yourself a hut elsewhere, away from the others, but it makes no difference – you witness the horrors of others and realize that the horror is also in you, it is you and what you are. And the whole grisly game is designed to keep you here, acting out that horror and even multiplying it by producing more and more people, for as long as possible.'

'What horrors?' he said. 'Your disgust at what you do shows that your nature is far better than you believe.'

'I mean the cruelty of which we are all capable, and which is evidence of the dreadful flaw in our design—'

'If we could be cruel but are not, surely that makes us so much better?

151

She shook her head against his chest. 'Even if we were to restrict ourselves for the rest of our lives, never killing or injuring another being, and living in solitude so that we could say and do nothing that would hurt another – even if we were to do that, it still could not prevent us from injuring ourselves with the thought of our death, our potential, our desires. We are by nature designed to harm, even if that harm is purely reflexive.'

He felt two drops, eyes' distance apart, fall on his chest. He did not know how to answer her or why he felt that he must, and so he slept, his lips touching the soft crown of her head.

A loud banging on the door woke him. He sat up hastily. The woman was gone and the uncurtained window radiant with sunlight. Ullmann wrapped the rough grey blanket about his waist and yanked open the door. A blunt-featured man in the colony's grey uniform stood outside wearing a bored, impatient expression. 'Ullmann, W.,' he said peremptorily. 'I'm your gang chief. You should be dressed by now.'

Incensed at being woken and spoken to in this way, Ullmann began to speak angrily. With a twitch of irritation, the man drew his arm back and punched Ullmann expertly on the jaw. Ullmann staggered backwards into the bed frame, and was silent. 'Get dressed and get moving, Ullmann W.!' the man bellowed. He turned on his heel and began walking away.

Ullmann drew on the grey uniform which had somehow replaced his suit and overcoat on the chair. He looked around for his personal effects – the wallet, spectacles, watch and notebook he remembered having the previous day, but they were gone. On the pillow were the soft depressions of two heads and single strand of the woman's hair. He realized that he did not know her name.

The gang chief hustled him towards the lip of the quarry, where four other men waited with a barrow full of picks and shovels. They were eating coarse bread and had a tin mug each of black tea. They looked at Ullmann without surprise or comment, but one handed him a piece of bread and a mug. With a shock, Ullmann realized it was the Stalin-moustached man from the reception.

'Hello,' Ullmann said uncertainly. 'This isn't quite what I expected of this morning.'

The man was about to answer when the gang chief bellowed at them to move off to the rock face. Two of the others made noises of displeasure but the group tipped up the barrow and began moving immediately. The moustached man muttered to Ullmann, 'Don't let him see us talking. He likes to lay about him with his fists.'

'I know,' said Ullmann. 'He punched me in the face when he came to wake me up this morning. I appreciate your attempt to immerse me in the life of the place, but I think I can observe and write my report dispassionately. I was extremely unhappy to be treated like one of the men. It rather neglects the fact that I haven't done anything wrong.'

'Of course, of course,' the moustached man said hastily. 'No one said that you had. But this is the way it is. Everyone has a chance when they arrive to make some observations, and these are taken in the spirit in which they're intended. But everyone must be prepared to work in whatever capacity is recognized, so that each person contributes to keeping the place going, filling it with workers, making those workers committed to the life of the place and so on.'

'But I'm not here to work like this!' said Ullmann. 'Last night you seemed to be in charge of the place! I saw you at the reception …you were wearing a suit – why, you made a speech of welcome and now here you are, hacking rocks! There's been some awful mistake. Neither of us is doing what we ought to be. There must be someone I can speak to.'

'Of course,' said the man. 'You can speak all you like – in a low voice, while you work at the rock, naturally. *I'm* interested in what you have to say.'

'But I'm not supposed to be doing this!' Ullmann shouted.

At once, the gang chief appeared, his fists clenched. 'Shut up, Ullmann W.,' he bawled. He looked derisively at Ullmann, who became aware that his uniform trousers were too short, leaving his ankles exposed. 'I knew you'd be a problem as soon as I laid eyes on you. Everything about you is entitled and bloody different. You're no different to anyone here, so get a shovel and get going!' He grabbed a shovel from the barrow and rammed it at Ullmann's chest before turning away. As he walked past one of the others in the gang he kicked him in the back of the leg. The man's legs buckled and he fell forward, striking his head against the sharp rock. He slid down it, face first, and lay unmoving.

'Keep shovelling,' the moustached man said. 'As long as you keep filling the barrow he doesn't really care what you do. You've just got to know him and how he works, if you see what I mean.'

'But…aren't you his superior?' said Ullmann in amazement.

'Only yesterday, and only in a manner of speaking,' the man said, swinging his pick against the rock. He made very little impression on it; almost nothing came off for Ullmann to shovel, but he made it look as though he was working extremely hard. To be doing something, Ullmann scraped about on the ground with the shovel, picking up small stones here and there and flipping them into the barrow. From a distance, he thought, it probably did look as if they were labouring away. 'What do you mean, only yesterday?'

'Oh, we've all welcomed new arrivals,' the other man said. 'Worn the suit and brought some new soul in. It's a job, like any other. Keeps the place going, which is the main thing.'

'But everyone's not the same!' said Ullmann. 'I mean, not everyone's here for the same reason!'

'Of course they are!' the man said, laughing as he swung the pick. 'In essence, we are all here for the same reason – to keep the place working, to make more of ourselves, and to experience being here.'

Ullmann began to suspect that he was the victim of a dreadful practical joke. He shovelled diligently for some time and tried to work out what to do. He wanted to see the woman again. She seemed the only sane person he had met, and as the sun grew brighter and his arms more tired, his body began to long for the moment he rested his lips in her hair and fell asleep with her weight and warmth around him. No matter how hard he tried to think of a solution, his body kept calling out for the rest and peace of the previous night.

He realized that he had no one to summon, and that his uncertainty about whence he had come and for what purpose meant that he could not express a preference for returning somewhere else. Whatever mistake or joke or trick he was stuck in would be his state until it pleased someone else to end it, or he began to prefer it of his own free will. He could not even leave the quarry, he saw, or the gang chief would bring him back and beat him. Worst of all, he could see that at some point he might be tasked with the gang chief's job and having to bellow at some other confused newcomer.

'It's unbelievable,' he said aloud. 'It's an absolutely bizarre way to run a prison.'

'A prison?' said the man with the moustache, who had halted his ineffectual hacking. 'Whatever makes you call it that?'

A Tour of Kinsella Mansion

He is wearing a cream summer suit with a 'pith hat'; he is every bit the private-schoolboy on his summer hols, resting in the shade, while in the background 'his' Arcadia glows in its fertile glory. Here is the granary of Empire, the wealth that keeps home secure.

John Kinsella, *Spatial Relations*

We agree: it's such a big place, this poetic mansion, that we can't visit all the rooms. We get the guidebook and choose a few poems: the word 'finches' tends to make us move on. You like people; I like wheat (well, bread, which is almost as good), so we agree to stop at poems which have people and wheat in them. After some reading, you say that you'll see 'After Sir Lawrence Alma-Tadema's *94° in the Shade* (1876)', the cheerful sounding 'Drowning in Wheat' and 'Anathalamion', if I'll see 'Hockney's Doll Boy at the Local Country Women's Association Annual Musical: Wheatbelt, Western Australia'.

It's a big place – more than fifty poems, although some of them are simply facades – like the doors in display homes which imply that an *en suite* bathroom or a walk-in closet lies behind them. (They turn out to be fake, two inches deep in the magnolia gyprock. The more elaborate the façade, the more likely it is to be churned out by some Chinese poetry factory. They take the measurements of better poems and do a good job at imitation, but there's always a comical error, something in the title that gives the ersatz-marble/genuine stucco away. They're the poetic equivalent of hotel instructions from Google translate: *Please make full use of Maid on Bed.*)

It's pretty clear from the start that this is a house of poetry you could only love if you were brought up in it. You enjoy it more than I can, because you were born hereabouts. Me, I'm from far away. I'm not even from this continent, and the poet's dislike of people from my part of the world becomes pretty clear on our very first stop.

There's a copy of Lawrence Alma-Tadema's *94° in the Shade* as we enter the poem, which is a kind of ekphrastic response to Alma-Tadema's painting. The poem feels like a feminist response to the Mona Lisa – a kind of sour rage at how contained she is in this male frame, with her annoying smile.

Anyway. In the painting we have a youth lying on his front, cheek in hand, reading a book on butterflies. His weapon is a butterfly net, cast to the side. He wears a horribly hot-looking suit, buttoned up over a shirt and tie and heavy black shoes. A pith sun cap, which young Winston Churchill might have worn as he escaped the Boers, sits on his undeniably British head. And perhaps it's because of the English setting – messy golden haystooks, the gentle, soaring sky of light cornflower blue, a low, near horizon that means small fields, a small country, aged and settled – Kinsella doesn't like the boy at all. He loads him down with that most Australian term of opprobrium:

He's confident. Maybe

overconfident.

There's absolutely nothing in the boy's manner (since we can't see his face, we can hardly tell from that) to suggest this. The

schoolboy on holidays, resting in the still shade,
confident within the granary of empire, wealth
that keeps home secure

is cast as a self-satisfied pommy twit, indulging his Fauntleroyian leisure before heading out to keep down the colonies. I stand in the middle of the piece, feeling very uncomfortable.

You protest that I'm being unkind. Why am I mooning over the clean, Insular sky that I understand, and fields growing a grain whose mysteries I know and revere? You sigh and grumble that I'm getting maudlin at the very beginning of our visit to Kinsella's poetic mansion. I say that I'm disappointed to be confronted by such unjustified dislike. Arrogance is a foolish thing of which to accuse someone, especially a talentless teenage lepidopterist in a painting. But the worst thing you can be in Australia is arrogant. And the builder of this poetic edifice, this bungalow-on-steroids, has levelled the deadly charge at an English boy, minding his own business a half-century and 12,000 miles away from Wheatbelt, Western Australia. To Kinsella the kid is still an overconfident son of empire, whose wealth and bookish leisure (arrogance!) are clearly the result of bleeding the colonies dry.

Now I'm uncomfortable. You drag me off, tell me we're going to look at 'Anathalamion'. It's got people *and* wheat, you say. It's got to be good. I'm uncomfortable now; the blatant antagonism of the last poem feels like a reminder that the place wasn't built for me, that I won't understand what I'm seeing. It's like low lintels; tall visitors feel as though they're subtly hostile.

We pass some cheerless reflections on cemeteries, dead birds, storms, a tiger hunt, and reach 'Anathalamion' by a back stair. I'm concerned that we're missing a vital element of sequence or story, but you point out that as long as we notice the repeated motifs, we've got the gist of the place. Salt, neglect, fallow fields, cutters, bullocks, various native bits of vocabulary, a place-name or two. Like curtain swags, they add gravitas to poetry reconstituted from an NRMA guidebook. Upcycled shabby-chic touches personalise a poetic McMansion.

'Anathalamion' is a squeeze cage of rural frustration, thirteen poems distant from the teenage butterfly-hunter. Feral kids, poisoned sheep, silos of wheat, angry, inarticulate parents and a man obsessed with a blue heron which he has too few words to describe.

The intellectual landscape is like Hieronymus Bosch – I think of Bosch's *Haywain* (circa 1516). A burning horizon terminates the familiar flat plain of damnation where weird, creeping things carry out unspeakable tortures in front of a ruined tower – or is it a silo? It's a choice between the heron-mad old man and some feral kids who kill the sheep, trap snakes, and steal dirt bikes. Remind me, I ask, why these little bastards, locusts in the fields, are regarded with affection, but the butterfly boy is 'overconfident'?

You reply that it's because we're looking at family photos in this poetry-house. The bungaloid Kinsella is one of the feral kids; this room's part-photo essay, part temple to nostalgia.

I still think 'Anathalamion' looks like Bosch's Haywain, perhaps because none of the kids regard this fearful world of burning brutality as abnormal. Wheatbelt, a monotony of grain without legend, is as bad as it gets. You need imagination to fear. The topography here is one of voids, blanks where things should be but are not. Ideas, revolutions, castles, creeds, exiles and exoduses, plans. Just the creeping things up and down the slow high street of their own madness, beneath strangled, hanging birds.

You get frustrated; there are other people in the poetry mansion, you say – *interesting* people. Look at that guy in 'Fruits of the Auger', holding the mangled stump of his arm! What more do you want – even the bloody auger's personified! Oh, I say, I thought that was a misprint. I thought it was an augur, *crazy with his blood*. That'd have been more interesting. But in a choice between augury and power-tools, I suppose Wheatbelt *would* go with the latter.

You're about to go and wait for me in the gift shop.

Look, you say, why don't we have a bit of fun. Let's bring the pith-helmeted boy into Wheatbelt. Introduce him to the sheep-poisoning feral kids. It happens, you know, still.

I know, I say acidly, it happened to *me*, remember?

Intrigued in spite of myself, I think about it. Like switching things in a stately home, putting Queen Victoria's knickers in the Prince Regent's bedroom. Just for fun. But I remind you that bringing folk from one work to another doesn't always end well. Remember the time we made Ferdinand see Caliban first, not Miranda? Love at first sight became distinctly uncomfortable.

You snigger. I say *Rebellious, migratory flights don't end up where they're supposed to, and water runs through the vista*. And tartly, you reply *Sometimes we coincide now more than ever*. See? you say, the poet *wants* to put the

159

butterfly boy in that squeeze cage of sun-stunned colonial kids. He *wants* to see the arrogance of empire get ripped to shreds.

I ask, on what earthly basis do you think that?

You say, who knows – maybe the poet was bullied by some British kid at school.

So we bring them together: ding-ding! In the blue corner, we have British Butterfly Boy! In the red corner we have Aussie Feral Kids. There they are, coinciding now. Coinciding hard, in the heavy chiaroscuro landscape of Kinsella's bungaloid world. *Lyrical disobedience?* Unlikely. The feral kids, who watched a sheep die *but didn't mean any harm* and lined the high street to watch the palsied misery of two old folk whom they'd driven to madness – what would they have done with Alma-Tadema's butterfly boy? What would he have done to them?

Feral kids are represented by Hockney, from the epically-named 'Hockney's Doll Boy at the Local Country Women's Association Annual Musical: Wheatbelt, Western Australia'. There're beery shouts and some thigh-slapping homophobia from rough-voiced good old boys. Hockney's the natural antagonist of Butterfly Boy, who just wants to be left with his net and book, to watch and wander a wholesome field, and pay in private ecstasy his reverences to the old gods of field and brook.

Butterfly and Hockney meet among the silo mouths, *potrait and landscape hang languidly about each other*. Hockney accuses him of being an arrogant, poofter pommy bastard. Butterfly stares out at the wheatfields, listens to them rattling in the wind, and knows that the rattle is the air playing in the wheat's armour of petrified silicic acid. He knows that this sound terrified the wild Germans when they stormed into the Roman Empire and heard the wind in a wheatfield for the first time. And he knows that the feral kids would hate him for knowing this, for finding it *in a book*. It offends him, that they live so well in a land of which they know nothing. They bleat and twitch the

160

curtains of their matchbox minds, beat and cajole him into being 'nice', being 'a good bloke'.

Butterfly Boy resents us, mischievous visitors in Kinsella Mansion, for transporting him from a corner of an English field, to a salt-soiled footnote of the ex-empire.

The feral kid, maddened by Butterfly's solitary, independent, literate, restrained, self, rush at him. Butterfly helps him over his ivory-suited hip, neatly pitching him through the dark mouth of the silo. Hoop-la! Feral hits the wheat with the sound of dry rice on a pavement.

No one can help him. Kinsella can't help him. He's busy in *Solitary Activities*, which Australians fear and suspect. Butterfly peers over the silo's edge; a glyphosate stink wafts up. Fluttering, frail, uncertain, Feral sinks beneath the waves of wheat. Agile rats scamper around him. He struggles in the ocean of plenty that he cannot understand or master, and drowns.

Happy now? you ask.

I suppose I am, I say, heading for the exit. Poetry has power, even collections subtitled 'Poms unwelcome'; 'Aussie poems for Aussie readers'. And when the reader invents a way of righting that balance, by mixing it up a little, by reading inventively, well – the poets must accept that, too.

I won't ask for my money back, but I won't visit again.

What Miss Mischa Knows

What cats don't know about the world isn't worth knowing. This applies to poetry as well, of which cats are a form. Miss Mischa, the cat in David Malouf's poem 'Eternal Moment at Poggia Madonna' tells us something valuable about cats and poetry, but it is something to which English teachers (who are often cat-lovers and poetry-lovers) might greatly object. Miss Mischa offers a lesson about discretion, and valour, and sleeping through things which are disagreeable and intractable.

How do you approach poetry? Is it reverently? Discretely? Affectionately but not familiarly? If so, then pass on – you are no fool, and the hour of my thoughts needs no guarding from you. Or do you do a fingertip trawl through each line? Do you crumble it apart like a dinner roll looking for similes and adjectival phrases? Do you lose the wood for the lexical trees until all that's left is a mess around the high-chair from which you've been spoon-feeding kids mashed-up verse? Is this vivisection of glittering moments how you pay your mortgage? Is the death of the poem a sad but necessary consequence of showing a class how it works?

You wouldn't do it to a cat, which nature has equipped with more defences than a poem. Why, then, do it to a poem? Behold Miss Mischa, whose essential nature cannot be separated from the elegance of her design, the integrity of each marvellous part. Does dissecting a cat's eye to identify the tapetum lucidum really explain the gleam of that wicked, knowing gaze in the dark? Malouf, himself a cat-like soul, writes as much about poetry as he does about Miss M. in 'Eternal Moment.' The *cool reclusion*, the presence of warmth across ages of human time, the immanent moments in which gods and matter meet – as with Miss Mischa, so with a poem.

Look at the picture of Miss Mischa in your mind's eye, curled around herself. Can you fix exactly where her sinuous spine ends and her tail begins? This is a trick – it's not just that you can't find that place; it's pointless to try. The attempt just shows how little you understand the nature of a cat.

The perfection of cats, like poems, has something to do with wholeness, completeness. In all cats and some very good poems, we can see Aristotle's definition of perfection: a thing so good that nothing of the kind could be better, and which has attained its purpose. The subtle and delicate elegance of Malouf's poem, which takes on the ineffable qualities of the cat, shows us the ugliness of the analytical position, and how the close reading habit serves only to break apart.

Certainly, there is always a sense of awe, even of jealousy, mixed into our curiosity about cats – perhaps it is the same for 'close readers'. Beneath our love for cats, our willingness to abase ourselves before their sometimes awful behaviour, is our belief that they know things that we do not, and a hope that at some point we may know it too. People who dislike cats resent this, and it may account for their dismissive remarks about it being 'just' a cat. The first step in loving a cat in the manner proper to them, is the same as loving poetry: it is the acknowledgment that you will never fully know its meaning, and are content to marvel at its design rather than fracture it. I wonder if Keats, with all his Negative Capability, liked cats.

Here is what we cannot say to people who have set up 'critical thinking' as their little godlet: most analysis is ugly, profane, and foolish. Be as the poet is to Miss Mischa; stand at a respectful distance and imagine the god bending down. Don't seek to put yourself between the fur and the divine fingertip, and certainly don't ask which god he is or how you spell his name. The cat within the poem within the cat – it is an infinite regression within which you are not wanted, because nature and the sacred mysteries do not wish to be spoken of openly and plainly.

Gettiered

...Again, Smith had a belief that was true and justified, but not knowledge.
Edmund L. Gettier, 'Is Justified True Belief Knowledge?'

I put the story in to Nicky's writing group and they tore it apart.

'It's based on nothing. It's about her *feeling* that it happened, which is a pretty poor foundation for a story,' Richard said. Richard had been retrenched from middle management. Most of his comments involved a lack of substance and strong foundations.

Rob waggled his fingers. In the stained Starbucks velvet armchair several spare tyres jiggled beneath his Wolfsbane t-shirt. 'It's women's stuff.' He remembered that his turn was coming up next week. 'It's just not my thing. If it's not genre, I'm not really interested. Sorry.' He reached for the tub of vanilla swill on the scarred table.

Hannah was working on a long-form life-writing mixed-voice piece which was a rehash of Jane Austen in the style of Jeanette Winterson. I liked Hannah, but I dreaded her stuff. It was a writers' group – nobody liked each other's stuff. 'Is it true? I mean, did it actually happen to you?'

Nicky said quickly, 'It doesn't matter if it's true. It had to be based on fact, but how you interpreted that was up to you. What's true, anyway? Everything has a truth in it, even things about wildly unsupported worlds.' Nicky's only published novel had been a thinly-disguised story about Nicky's affair with one of his graduate students, which had led to Mrs Nicky trying to off herself in Nicky's office. This had in turn led to the end of Nicky's nascent academic career, and his transference to Starbucks in Hampstead, where he ran writing groups for the undiscovered and unpublishable.

Sarah, who freely admitted she was writing through mother-issues, said, 'I'm never *comfortable* when we persecute the old. I mean, how she dealt with his dementia was up to her, but to make him a *murderer* on the basis of a single snapshot…it just seems, well, *mean.*'

Nicky disliked the lack of closure. 'Call me old-fashioned, and I really *get* that life's like that, with things just tailing off, but…I don't know. It felt so undecided.' He gave me a comforting smile. 'But there was a lot to like, Kate, there really was.' I had a feeling that Nicky was hoping to make me the next nail in Mrs Nicky's coffin, so I studied my story and tried to bounce back the beady radiance of his smile.

In fact, it *was* true – and based on facts, or real, or whatever you wanted to call it. It had happened.

I had been the last passenger on the bus as it bumped up Fleet Road to the little terminus at South End Green. I looked down as I was getting off and saw a brown leather wallet on the step. I was about to hand it to the driver when he yelled at me to get a move on. It was a hot, dirty London summer and the driver had dealt with several lost and noisy Brazilian tourists. I'd only get the rough edge of things if I saddled him with lost property, so I pocketed it and hopped off.

That evening, I looked through it properly. It was a man's wallet; gold initials on the corner had been worn down to one leg of an *H*. There was a £20 note, an Oyster card, and a Natwest bank card – without a chip – with the name William R. Heble on it. A library card for Camden Council libraries and a British Library reader's ticket, now four years out of date, with a photo of a man in his seventies.

I was mildly surprised to find a W.R. Heble listed in the phone book, around the corner at Mansfield Road. I was going to run out and drop the wallet through their letter box when I felt a zip at the back of the long horizontal pocket. I unzipped it and saw a very creased photograph, turning that red-brown colour that old photos do when acid begins to fade the inks and eat through the paper. I pulled it out carefully. It was a head-and-shoulders shot of a little boy, maybe five or six years old, beneath a cloudless blue sky. There was an out-of-focus blue glistening space behind him which suggested the sea, and a beigey blur of sandstone on one side.

There's nothing really in it, I suppose. *Pace* Nicky, stories are supposed to be about a conflict: Man vs Man (or woman), Man vs Nature, Man vs Self. This central conflict causes the story-world to destruct, recombine, and continue anew through the synthesis of now-resolved elements. Without it there's just monotony. But if there was a conflict here I can't see it. It's just the story of a moment of absolute certainty. I knew something, in that sense that knowledge is justified true belief. When Nicky told us to write about something based on fact, I wrote about this moment in which I believed something about an event in the world, and I had reasons to justify that belief.

It was the look on the boy's face – a look of absolute horror, the look you might give when you see a car about to hit you, or the train that you're about to fall under. Possibly if a scientist were to examine the picture, they'd say that I had subconsciously recognized that the angle of the boy's bare shoulders to the camera was dangerous. That intuitively I knew he was falling backwards as the shutter clicked, capturing the look of terror, of the horror of death and falling from that sun-bright cliff.

It was an awful image. I think I dropped it and sat for a few minutes just wishing I hadn't seen it; trying to bend the muscles of my everyday brain around this outsize fact. After a minute, I turned it over. In very faint pencil someone had written *T, West Bay, July '77*.

Other people would have questioned my belief that the photo showed the boy falling backwards over a sea cliff – or more precisely, being pushed off a cliff by the very person holding the camera. Or admitted that, while it *was* a strange picture, there was no reason to believe that it showed the boy on the point of a horrible death. They would have returned the wallet and forgotten about it.

But the contour of stories doesn't match the shape of lived events. What I've told you is the whole story – the opening action, the climax, the resolution. Even the falling action is unremarkable: the next day I went round to the Mansfield Road address, which was a nice terrace in South-East England Gloomy Elegance style, with expensive drapes and two potted standard fuchsias and ivy flanking the front door. A woman in her early fifties, wearing the South-East England Gloomy Elegance uniform of silk blouse, statement necklace, Italian shoes and ash-blonde hairdressered hair, came to the door. I explained that I lived on Fleet Road and had found the wallet on the bus. As I was speaking, a man, whom I dimly remembered being on the bus, came up behind her.

'It's my father's wallet,' the woman said. She took it from me and gave it to the old man. 'Put it in your pocket, Dad. This young woman found it on the bus where you'd dropped it.' She said this in the unnaturally loud voice adult children use to let the world know they've been saddled with aged parents.

Mr Heble was tall, mild-looking, and cardiganed. He could once have been anything. It was difficult to imagine him pushing a small boy to his death while taking a souvenir photo. Mr Heble thanked me very much, pocketed his wallet, and pottered away. The daughter leaned out of the doorway and said, 'He's eighty-six and has dementia. At least he didn't lose himself this time.' She straightened and said more loudly, 'Thank you so much.' And shut the door.

I went down the steps wondering what I'd expected. Bill Sykes? An eye patch and a cudgel? I had looked into Mr Heble's rheumy blue eyes and seen nothing. Cells dying behind them and a watery blur of memory. He probably didn't even remember who the child T was, or what had happened that day at West Bay forty years before.

This, I suppose, is why Nicky and the others found it unsatisfying. But there are only a few other ways to proceed after that. One is outwards, to the people involved: what about me? What makes me the kind of person who sees such things in chance-found photos? Or Mr Heble – what was he like before he became a walking vessel of neural plaque, living in an eternal present? Or daughter Heble, who hadn't even given me her name. What, if anything, did she remember about *T.* and a hot summer holiday in her early teens? Any one of these could have carried this nodule of narrative forward, into a full-blown P.D. James-cum-Mary-Wesley story. South-East England well-educated longing and repressed anger, buttoned into a cashmere cardigan.

A month or so went by, during which I joined Nicky's group of scribblers and sat a lot in Starbucks, wondering whether my husband was coming back from Alaska, or Hong Kong, or wherever he was being consulted about mysterious business processes. I tried – we all tried, in the group – to observe other people as characters, to take notes about human motivations and quirks of speech which we would turn into beautifully rounded studies of humanity in our literary bestsellers. It was mostly nonsense. You write because there's something you want to get off your chest, and it involves particular people, whom you don't need to observe because you've been marked indelibly by them. The observing and notebooking is just pomp covering up a purposeless solitude.

As I said, the group didn't like the piece. So much for Eliot's 'still point' of absolute certainty. I should have shown them the photo and said, 'Tell me I'm wrong about this picture.' Because I had kept it. I don't really know why. I had no reasons for wanting it, since it had genuinely upset me. I didn't plan to look at it again, and I don't think I wanted to show it to anyone else. Maybe my husband, when and if he ever drifted back.

A couple of weeks after my literary disappointment, Mr Heble came to my flat. He was alone, which surprised me, and in shirtsleeves, which I thought meant that he was out without the daughter's knowledge. I invited him in.

'I saw you come out of the delicatessen,' he said. 'I remembered the wallet. You brought it back last week.'

I didn't mention that it had been six weeks previously. 'You do have a good memory for faces,' I said. 'I doubt if I could remember someone from last week.' I was conscious of speaking to him like a child, but it's a habit we fall into when we think someone isn't quite the full shilling. He sat on the sofa and smiled peacefully. I made us a cup of tea and sat opposite him. 'So what brings you to see me?'

He took a sip of tea. 'You have something of mine. From my wallet.'

In the fractional silence which followed, I compared the directness of his address, how purposeful he sounded, with his apparent inability to remember how long ago he lost the wallet.

'Oh,' I said, trying to sound neutral. 'What was it?'

He gave a small smile. 'A photograph.'

Under any other circumstances, I would have said it was impossible to tell that Mr Heble had dementia, but what we know – or believe we know – gives texture to the world in which we act. Knowing informs doing.

'A photograph of what?'

'Of my son Tom,' he said. There was something slightly unfocused about his gaze. Despite his lucidity, his eyes still had the blurry quality of old age, as though he was looking past me.

'I think I remember a photo,' I saw, wondering how far I could draw him out. Although he was a good six inches taller than me, he had taken care sitting down, and his feet had the awkward position of someone who doesn't feel quite connected to them. 'A little boy.' I took a breath. 'Yes – it looked as if he was falling backwards.'

'Ah.' Mr Heble sat back on the sofa and looked at me with a kind of appraisal. 'Yes. It was taken as—' I realized I was holding my breath. 'Do you have it? I'm anxious to have it back. He died, you see, and it's the last picture we have of him.'

I saw that he wasn't going to be explicit about anything until he had the photo in his hand. 'I took the things out of your wallet at my desk,' I said, trying to sound relaxed. 'Let me go and look.'

I went into my small study and made a racket opening and closing drawers. The photo was in a pile of papers I was avoiding for one

170

reason or another. I looked at it again. The look on the boy's face was unmistakeable – horror, terror, and the shock you only ever see when someone is falling, falling perhaps mortally.

I took it out to him. 'It was in my desk,' I said. I sounded unconvincing.

He took it and looked fondly at the boy. I was afraid he would leave without saying anything else. 'He doesn't look…happy,' I said. There was a pause. 'You said he died that year? He was very young. I'm sorry.' Another pause.

'I'm glad to have it back,' he said. He ran a thumb over the cracked surface. 'It's all I have of that day.'

'That wasn't the day he died was it?' I took a breath. 'It wasn't taken…'

He looked at me sideways, the way a bird looks at you before swiping something from your plate. Bright-eyed and knowing and not quite human. Or perhaps it was completely human. It wasn't a nice look to have cast on you, in a flat, alone, even with the racket of North London traffic outside. 'It wasn't,' I whispered.

'As he died,' he said. 'He died. That year. And we'd had such a nice holiday. The sand there – it's so fine. You'd have to go to the Hebrides for sand that fine in the rest of Great Britain.'

I felt like shouting at him. I stared into the corner and tried to get a grip. What had he told me? What was it that I knew? 'Would you like to walk me home?' he said suddenly. 'I'm not…the way back seems to have escaped me.'

I looked at him. An old man who couldn't remember his own way home, whom I was painting a child-killer in my head. I suddenly cursed my husband for being away. 'Yes, of course,' I said. 'Let me get my bag.'

I had turned my back when he spoke again. 'As he went over, you know, he said *Oh Dad*. It was so…so satisfying.'

I paused long enough for regret to strike me like a kettlebell. And then I got my bag.

His daughter was extremely relieved. 'First his wallet and now the whole man,' she said. 'Dad, this is just...' she seemed genuinely lost for words of complaint, which was unusual for Englishwomen. Her father smiled mildly and drifted into the depths of the house. 'Thank you again,' she said. 'It's really getting a bit out of hand. We don't know how long he can stay at home, but...'.

'I understand,' I said, though I didn't. 'It's your father.' I was about to turn and go, but I wanted some kind of sanity check. 'Your father was telling me about your brother. He said he had died in 1977.' I didn't mention the photograph.

She looked surprised and then slightly shocked. I steeled myself. 'It's funny, isn't it,' she said slowly, 'what they remember. So long ago, and Tom was so young.' She made a twist of her mouth. 'Well. It was 1977. They couldn't treat leukaemia the way they can now.'

'Leukaemia?' I'd blurted it out before I could stop myself. 'I'm sorry...I thought...your father gave me the impression that your brother died in an accident. A fall at the seaside.'

She looked at me oddly. 'No, no. It was childhood leukaemia. Very quick – well, comparatively. We came back from holiday and Tommy started to feel sick. Tired. You know, the early symptoms. He was gone by Christmas.'

'God, I'm so sorry,' I said. There was an uncomfortable pause. 'Well, I'll let you get on.'

What you probably want to know is – did it really happen this way, or did I invent some closure for my first, unsatisfying attempt to write an account of it? You can't be sure. At some point, when my memory has become like William Heble's, I won't be sure either. When we subject knowledge to really close scrutiny, it becomes unstable, like a con-artist who's been cornered.

That photo wasn't a record of Tom Heble's death; but I still knew something about it. I knew that his father had, *in some way*, or perhaps in some universe, killed Tom. For the space of only a shutter click, forty years previously, my belief was justified and true – it was

172

knowledge – even if it only obtained in the private universe of someone else's head. Writing of what we know, and the circumstances of knowing it, frequently provides no greater closure than the wildest speculations – if there is any real difference between them.

How Beautiful, How Good to Eat

One evening, when they were all sitting round the camp fire and the sunset was blazing over the Thessalian hills, Orlando exclaimed: 'How good to eat!'
(The gipsies have no word for 'beautiful'. This is the nearest.)
Virginia Woolf, *Orlando*

They ate the last of the meat on Saturday. The men sailed on the Sabbath with the outgoing tide, and the minister shouted at them silently from the headland. The women had emasculated him long ago. They stood on the beach and watched the brown boats until the outgoing tide turned, then picked up their cockling-creels, all lipless, silent, black as crows, rough as stone-washed rocks.

By noon the day was white-hot. The sea steamed and turned like boiling paint. The gulls baked their membranous feet on the rocks, uncatchable since there would be no meat eaten until the fleet returned. Cockling, the women called to each other in their own tongue, the one reserved for wash days and the fleet's absence, and they sounded like gulls themselves. Harsh fingers gestured to harsh mouths where the harshest sounds came out. And as they called and cawed, he floated towards them on the turning tide. This was how he came to the island; as shipwrecked, sodden and near dead as a man could be, cast up on the white stones. And the women wheeled and cawed around him, gazing at his sodden clothes, his outflung arm, his sailor's head resting face down on the shore.

He was not one of their men, and so they took him up and turned him. One of their own foolish enough to be cast overboard, to let the sea snatch him so soon, would have been left for dead by the women he had failed. But a stranger can only be judged by his own people, so the oldest woman took the sodden arm and rolled him onto his back like a baby. And for one look at his face the women were silent, and the day boiled more tightly, and the birds on the rocks scorched their feet. And they all, even the day itself, had the same thought. Who could not have loved this sailor? He was brown – there are no other kinds of men in the world – and black haired, and had as tight and straight a mouth as a boat. The planes of his face were like new wood, not the driftwood-gnarled wandering of their own men's skin. His arm was solid as a mast. His eyebrows were the exact shape of a gull's wing, and as long, as sharp, as clear against the sky.

They woke him up by pressing hard on his chest, and he spat up brine like a baby onto the oldest woman's shoulder. One woman removed her clothes and dressed him in them and then crouched, brown and naked, as the others mumbled and turned over the soil in their minds like earthworms, letting this new thing in. He mewled and huffed like the minister's cat and a young mother gave him her milky breast there on the shore, and he suckled sleepily. And they all had the same thought.

So they picked him up between them and carried him on the cockling creels like a bier to the youngest woman's house. The minister stood on the machair before his big white house and screamed a tongueless warning to the sailor and the women. No one heeded his cries and eventually the gulls came and picked off some more of his white bone and black cloth.

The sailor's shoulders were wider than the lintel above the doorway and the women paused for a moment, considering the strength of his bones and how a house for many generations could be built from them. So they took him to another house, where he only just fitted, and stripped him of the woman's clothes. The smell of so much sea was dizzying. It made the women flush with longing for earlier times, when they preened their blubber and oily skin on warm, wet rocks. To wash the sea's immensity from him they brought a great stone pot and placed him in it, naked as a whelk in its shell. A young wife, spectacular and naked, climbed into the pot with him and washed him with her hair and feet and the palms of her hand, rougher than a pumice stone. And the other women stood around, gazing at

175

his muscular hardness, the goodness in the flesh beneath the water, and hungered for him.

Under all this the sailor was silent and dutiful. He did not speak the language of the women, but he knew of the islands in the farthest part of the sea, and the people like bleached driftwood who lived there. He heard the women's mumbling as the naked one passed her hard hands over his shoulders, down his belly, even seeking out the brine behind his ears. In their absolute bareness they had no peat, no clay, no paper. They traded for metal and made everything out of the rawest substances, even their men, even their words. His skipper once told him that they had no concept of image, and could not fashion a likeness of a man, but that they saw likeness between all men and things. He said that the women mated indiscriminately with men and seals, and that the old had the life beaten out of them so that they could die with dignity. They had no concept of beauty, no word for beautiful, but said rather that something was good to eat. These and many more things passed through the sailor's mind as he was washed clean amid so much water and stone. The women anointed him with rock salt, subtly, and machair-grass. And they licked every inch of him to work in the salt and smoky greens.

They had no clothes in which to put him, and no table at which to serve him. So they laid him naked on the bed, a great flat rock covered with the smoothest sealskin. They strewed peat flowers and machair grass around him and pressed him back on the bed, mumbling to him to be at ease, wondering at his beauty.

A kettle of sweet golden nettles was boiled, and threshed heads of marram grass were made into a gruel in stone bowls. They brought the last of the salt fish and a bowl of seabird's blood, still smelling of great heights, and placed it all around him, gesturing both at him and at the food. How beautiful, they murmured, how good to eat. And the sailor lay back, surrounded by the strewing flowers and smiled back at their shy offerings. So must Odysseus have felt, he thought, upon reaching Circe's island. What need has a man of a crew when he is

176

treated like a king? The women touched him, tentatively, anointing his feet and arms, the hollow of his collar-bones, with the food-offerings. How beautiful, they murmured, touching him. How good to eat, they whispered, shyly pushing the golden broth and stone-grey gruel before him.

The sailor ate some of the food, pleasing the women greatly, for they nodded, murmuring to each other and patting his naked belly. The sailor held out the salt fish to them and they came close to his couch, eying his beauty. They removed their clothes to save the soft-washed, powdery, many-times-pounded cloth, and sat around him, naked and soughing like an autumn field. They sailor looked at their gnarled magnificence like so many silent thoughts in the hut, and he thought how strange that they had no word for beautiful, but rather only 'good to eat'. He held out a piece of fish to a young woman and pointed to her, saying, 'How beautiful'. And the young woman crawled near and took the fish, saying, 'Yes, how good to eat'. And she bent over his throat, smiling shyly, and his whole heart was in his mouth. She bit and his blood flowed, and the women's hunger was released. All over him they crowded, tearing at the anointed flesh, like gannets, soaking up the sailor's salt-marinated blood, inhaling the scent of the sea's unexpected harvest. How beautiful! They murmured. How good to eat! And amid his strewing herbs, the sailor blinked dazedly.

A Last Walk in Marengo

Mother deceased. Funeral tomorrow. Faithfully yours.
Albert Camus, *L'Étranger*

I died today. Or perhaps it was yesterday; I can't be sure. Apart from a slightly greater physical restriction than I've had in the last few years, nothing much has changed. You spend a lifetime wondering what your last journey will be. The sheer scale of the thought frightens you into behaving well for your entire life – and it turns out to be a walk along the same road you went down with a friend just the other day, only this time you're being carried. If I'd known it was going to be so prosaic, I'd have misbehaved more.

On the whole, I'm not sorry to have died. Life was generally hard and tiring, although it became a lot more pleasant when we left France and returned to Algeria. Before money became too tight for his studies, I used to listen to my son talking about the philosophy he was reading, different theories about the value of life, how you're supposed to live it, the obligations you have to others and so on. Men can afford to see life in these theoretical terms; for women, a great deal of this life is taken up with how long socks take to dry. No, even in warm Algiers life was anxiety, and exhaustion, then finally sun, heat and a permanent doze which surpassed boredom. It was marriage, a child, widowhood, poverty, a few brief affairs to pass the time, and then the realization that my son Henri wished me gone from the apartment, and my own inability to think of a single reason not to oblige him.

Don't get me wrong, I did things that other people would call misbehaving. Everyone does; it's why we disapprove of other people. We don't disapprove of what they've done, but that they've been careless enough to make it common knowledge. Immorality is nobody's business - it's between you and God, if you believe in that

178

kind of thing – but carelessness is. That shows that you don't bother with the illusions which prop other people up and which, indirectly, keep society humming along.

I doubt that my dalliances with old Salamano, or my irritation with the priest who visited the Home at Marengo, really bothered anyone but why risk a peaceful existence just to affront people who matter as little as you do? And wasn't just a fear of rejection or a love of the unwritten rules for their own sake that made me discrete, but a selfish appreciation of what the machine oiled by those rules gets you. I liked fresh bread, fish on Fridays, cafés on the esplanade – all owned by people who experience the same boredom and anxiety as me. They manage because it's not being shoved in their face that I spent a warm afternoon making love to my upstairs neighbour, or laughed in the face of the priest whose logic is as kinked as his hair. We can put up with a great deal – that is to say, we can keep producing bread, and coffee, and fish, and cleaning other people's houses, and serving them in shops – if we believe that we're all suffering under the same restrictions.

This, of course, will be my son's problem. He's young and self-sufficient now. He can afford to ignore the fact that the world runs like an intricate clock, every spring balancing a load of spite and exhaustion. It takes only a day's failure to wind it and the whole thing stops and turns against you.

Guillaume understood. Both of us were shoved in Marengo by children we shouldn't have had, who were now impatient with our age and weakness. I cried a bit when Henri brought me here, more to see what it would achieve, but I didn't really mind. It's fine in the sun; the staff are pleasant enough, and any amount of bad behaviour is excused as old age and tiredness.

I can hear Guillaume, somewhere at the back of my little procession, dragging his bad leg. We tried to make love once, in the limited privacy allowed to the old, but neither of us were really interested. It's the kind of exercise that makes you co-ordinate manners and actions and appearance, like successful dancing. In the end we lay still and held hands and watched the shadows of the geraniums dance on the wall. We talked about the others at the Home and laughed. That's the secret – find someone with whom you can laugh at the world, and the rest of the time just stay silent. Silence, particularly for women, is a wonderful respite – any amount of scorn, loathing, confusion, and desire can be felt without consequence if you just stay silent.

No, I'm not sorry to have died, because it was all becoming very draining, what with having to pretend and prop up everyone else's beliefs all the time. When you realize you're dying there's a brief, momentary panic, but you shrug it off when you consider that it's already happening and it hasn't been so bad yet. You cling onto life more from boredom and a kind of politeness – you don't want to make your friends feel you're fleeing the very condition they think is worth so much. But at the last minute, when the breath is rattling in your chest like broken glass in a bucket, you're quite glad to let it go and jettison the condition to which you've always felt something of an outsider.

Soldier of Future Time

How queer and foreign it must seem to you and all the coarse words and cruelty which I now relate are far away in ancient time.
    Peter Carey, *The True History of the Kelly Gang*

In the newspaper picture my father is an empty iron suit, a trash-can of quarter-inch metal as crude and dented as a hobo's cup. I have pasted a clipping of this pitiful thing (threatening all the same) on the front of his manuscript. And kicked it under the bed in anger. I cannot kick it any further for the bed is up against the wall and if I sent the package of hooch-sodden excuses and poor Paddy poetry downwards into Conway Street, I would only be showing that I have inherited his temper.

The newspaper shows a dent at the right temple of the helmet, and one on the left cheek, two on either side of the breast, one athwart the ribs and another, which has pierced the plate, just above the appendix. Sadly, there is not a single dent in the rectangular plate looped over his waist and below. I quite like the image, for it makes me feel less aggrieved to think that there was clearly at least one person other than myself who wanted to wound Edward Kelly in each place I would have.

A trash can on his head! It covers his ears (his eyes are left visible through a slit like a letter box), his mouth and nose. So he could not hear or speak to the woman he abandoned, if she cried out to him as she does, all day and far, far into the night. He could not smell her, wasting and rotting as she feeds a cancer (newer than the one that settled in her heart when she sailed to the Americas from Port Melbourne), a cancer I cannot stop or treat.

'How queer and foreign it must seem to you,' he writes, *'and all the coarse words and cruelty which I now relate are far away in ancient time.'* It is wonderful to be addressed as some kind of bucolic fool, reading his

bag of similes and wind in my bower, swinging on a flower-decked loveseat and ordering tea! Wonderful in particular when the writer of this steaming pile of self-pity and paper heroism is the father who delivered himself of me and fled.

Perhaps I should have read the thing when I was less tired. We strive to be the readers our authors hope for - that much is just good manners. What did Edward Kelly hope for in the daughter to whom he writes? Sympathy, for certain. Sympathy for poverty and the bad, wild blood of the pagan Irish who landed in that forsaken scrub continent after the old world had jettisoned them.

But *we're* not poor. We're not rich either, but we're not poor, nor wild, nor angry, nor wily. We work hard and when someone above us - which in this country just means someone with more money - tries to profit themselves at our expense, we shake the dust off our feet and take our labour and our business elsewhere. This is America.

And yet. And yet. I've seen a roan mare in a shaft of sunlight, prancing under some richer woman who can't handle her, and my blood has played a rare reel in my veins and I've met that great rolling eye with my own and felt light-fingered for the bridle. But I turn away and head back indoors and stamp out the ghost of Kelly and all his charm and lying promises that lead to the gallows. I blacklead the fireplace. Again.

It's a terrible thing to distrust your own blood.

I see it in Mama, as death creeps up all over her, loosening her holding knots from within, making her less than a pile of leaves. It's the blood. Riot and debauch, shock-and-ride-away blood, the singing-in-the-gutter-of-a-Monday-night blood that is nothing but an inconvenience. Mama rages and lies, weeps and laughs, roils in her bedsheets and sweats like a bubbling pot and I know that it's the cancer but I also know that it's the ghost of Kelly calling her across years and oceans and desertion and death, and d--- the woman, but she'll never leave off loving him.

She looked at the clipping - I showed it to her after I pasted it on the cardboard cover of his manuscript - and even though she was twisted up in pain like a sheet going through the mangle, she laughed. It was like a girl's laugh, but something else as well - something dreadful and forlorn. Wind playing across the lip of an empty bottle. I was angry with her and said, 'Can't you see it for what it is? The cold empty shell of an eejit who reckoned he could bypass his crimes with this... this charade of armour!'

I was so angry at her for laughing (at me, I thought), that I tossed the thing onto the floor as if it were a rag. It spilled open and all the pages were strewn across the boards like so many fliers for the cheap Chinese shops on the quay.

When I came back, sorrowful and ashamed, she had hauled herself out of bed to gather the leaves together and hold them close with a shaking hand. I cannot get the picture of it out of my head, for it shows how terrible is love, and why I do not want it, nor shall ever have it near me. Eaten with cancer and years, she held that package of excuses closer to her heart than she could have held me, and she longed for him - I saw it, plain and clear and terrible - longed for her lying, horse-stealing, pitiful and penurious husband, my hanged father, Edward Kelly.

I will stop this. Ned Kelly and all his lies are no more to me than the wind and darkness inside his empty iron suit.

Viva Voce

Twice before, a book had turned him inside out and altered who he was, had blasted apart his assumptions about the world and thrust him onto a new ground where everything in the world suddenly looked different — and would remain different for the rest of time, for as long as he himself went on living in time and occupied space in the world.

Paul Auster, *4 3 2 1*

'Very interesting, Mr Auster,' the chairman said. 'And an excellent start to your rehabilitation, I think.' He beamed at Auster, who sat nervously on the plain hard chair at a great distance from the panel. His paragraph glared at him from a screen over the three doctors' heads.

'If I could begin?' the chairman said, looking at his two colleagues. They nodded and he faced Auster again, sitting pale-faced in the patient's chair. 'Here is our problem. This Auster-on-paper whom you claim is the 'real' you, the true and authentic Paul Auster – far more the real man than the flesh and blood creature sitting before us – what does he suffer from and how can we help him?'

Auster blinked and nodded, licking his lips in case he was called to speak. Having read his extract aloud he felt exhausted. He hoped it would prove helpful in his treatment.

'Now, it seems that in the paper Auster claims to have suffered three great shocks. Psychic shocks presented in the form of books he's read, which have revealed some falsehood in his view of the world.'

Auster nodded again. He recalled the first book – his first attack – and felt the tears start up.

'But,' the lady on the chairman's right continued kindly – so kindly that Auster wanted to weep and crawl over to her, to bury his face in her kind, kind lap and let her mother him until he felt better -

'but really the problem begins a little further back the chain. Let's look more closely at this passage, Paul. Would you like to do that?'

'Yes—' he mumbled, his teary-wet mouth wrapping itself around the word. 'Oh, yes.'

'Well,' she said, 'someone who has been turned inside out – you poor soul, it must have felt dreadful. Absolutely horrid! Someone like that has been completely altered from the normal, haven't they?'

Recalling it, Auster nodded vociferously. At last, someone understood. Someone sympathized.

'But you don't *need* to say that they're altered, do you?' she said, a little reprovingly. 'You've already said they've been turned inside out. So we could remove one or the other. Half the sentence.'

He saw what she meant and blushed. On the screen overhead she deftly deleted half the sentence.

'We've got a similar problem with the next bit,' said the man on the chairman's other side. 'I mean, if you've had your assumptions blasted apart, then evidently, the blast wave has moved you to new ground, eh? And if you change place, well – things naturally look different, don't they?'

'That's true,' said Auster, beginning to feel more hopeful.

'So we could probably get rid of the stuff after the blasting bit.' It was deleted.

'*Blasting* – it's a bit hyperbolic, isn't it? I mean, you've had the benefit of a modern education. Critical thought and all that. You shouldn't have *had* any assumptions so sturdy that they needed blasting. Might get rid of that too, eh?'

Auster shook his head in shame. He had known that the treatment was hard at the Derrida clinic, but this was… no, he shook it away. These people were professionals. They cared. They cared *for him*.

'As for the last part,' the lady resumed, 'we've dealt with your hyperbole and redundancy in one place and they break out in another.' She wagged a finger at him. She was beautiful, Auster thought dreamily. If he could imagine an ideal reader, she would be it. 'How do you live, except in time and space?'

There was a dreadful, mortifying silence. Auster shook his head again and looked at his knees.

'Shall we…?'

He burst into tears and covered his face with his hands. 'Cut it,' he said through his fingers. 'Cut it all.'

When he looked up, sniffing, the text on the overhead screen read only *Twice before, a book.* Three faces looked at him with parental concern.

'Much better, I think, Mr Auster,' the chairman said. His voice seemed to come from a long way away. 'We've solved the problem of your shock. And into the bargain we've solved the problem of you, too. A sentence needs a subject, and an author only exists as the writing subject. We've excised the word and the voice behind it, haven't we?'

But Auster was no longer there.

Ekphrasis: Chernobyl Liquidator

You know this image of the liquidator pushing the baby carriage. It is a picture of a man but it has clearly come from a time when we stopped being men and took on the nature of gods or devils. This man (or god, or devil) and what he pushes in the carriage, is part of history.

So, walking down the road of history comes a man in a radiation suit – booties covering his shoes, thick gloves on his hands, gas mask covering his face. There is a diagonal stripe across his chest which must belong to a respirator slung behind his back. Not only is he faceless – nose elongated in hideous, ridiculous proportions to the double-nozzle of the mask – but he is shapeless too. His two-piece protective suit has a rubbery sheen to it, even in the black and white of the image. He looks as if he has escaped from an asylum into an even madder countryside.

His hands are on the handle of a pram, one of the old-fashioned ones where the baby lies facing you, so you can watch it all the time. He is pushing the pram down a road and the sun shines behind them. It is a fractured version of the fairytale witch, come to take away the baby princess and bring her up in the wood, ignorant of her birthright.

The sun would be falling on the baby in the pram if he weren't blocking it. I'm assuming there's a baby in the pram because why else, in this clearly risky place, would he be pushing it? Some say that he is simply using the baby carriage to haul equipment, but the shadow, the possibility of the baby is still there. Uncovered, unmasked, its skin exposed to whatever even the man's skin cannot bear.

The truth of the image and the suggestion it makes in our imaginations are different but equally terrible. A man, pushing a baby carriage in the sunshine, in a place too poisoned for even a bare face – that's terrible enough.

He's looking at the imaginary baby as he pushes the pram. You can tell, from the slight downward tilt of his masked face, and the angle of the obscene google-eyes in his helmeted head, that he's riveted by the contents of the pram.

Perhaps it's because there's nothing else around to keep his attention; no other people, no vehicles, nothing. The crops standing high in the fields look withered, even scorched. There are leafless trees in the background. An empty meadow in what any encyclopaedia, history book, science textbook, will tell you was a beautiful May in 1986

History, in a thousand, billion, irradiated atoms, starting its long half-life.

We are all Ai Wei Wei

You're meeting Ai Weiwei. You're quite excited – this is the guy whose imprisonment by the Chinese Communist Party stirred the U.S. and European Union to protest, and caused the Tate Modern to write *Release Ai Weiwei* on their exterior. You're thinking that, if he'll say enough (and not in the cryptic, sloganish way of Ai's tweets, but in the helpfully extended, narrative way that artists like Chagall discussed their art) you'll have material for a short story, maybe even two. You plan to send it to the *New Yorker*, or *Harper's*, or perhaps even *Granta* if postmodern fiction about a postmodern artist isn't now too passé for them. You make a note to find out the age of their fiction editors – between 40 and 60 is ideal. You're thinking of a two-character piece about a writer (you) and an artist (Ai). Maybe you'll call it something like *I was Ai Weiwei*, in which the two characters meet at a retrospective of the artist's work.

Stories still have to be *about* something, though. OK, you think. So maybe the two characters steal one of the pieces. Maybe Ai Weiwei steals an Ai Weiwei. Can you steal your own work? Given the prestige apparently attached simply to *being* Ai Weiwei, could he actually steal? Or has his role as the political truth-teller elevated him to a level of fame and artistic suffering which makes him immune to law in the West?

What would the other character (you), be doing?

You're thinking about this as you wait for Ai, wandering through the retrospective. 100 million handmade, painted ceramic sunflower seeds made by 1600 artisans in Jingdezhen. You wander if each artisan got paid 1600th of what Ai has made from this phenomenally successful installation. Do they get 1/1600th of the *auteur*-worship from the black-turtleneck-wearing visitors to these exhibitions? Why isn't the piece credited to 'Ai Weiwei et al.'?

You make a mental note to ask him, when he shows up.

Thinking about this problem – of an artist who seems to use other, anonymized hordes of artisans to execute his work – you briefly consider calling the story *We are all Ai Weiwei*. That would probably go down better with a magazine. It's more *inclusive*; it suggests that the journal-reading graduates with software-salary politics are also suffering artists. Warm inclusivity *sells*.

You're getting fed up with his non-appearance. You go through other exhibits – 1300 bicycles, 3200 porcelain crabs, 32 sawed-up Qing dynasty stools, a 60-meter rubber boat with hundreds of rubber refugees – and fleetingly think that if you scale anything up enough it seems to make a statement. Even if it's just about How Stuff Fills Space. Coat it in matte gold or black latex and it's Definitely Art.

You check your watch. Where is this artist, whose concepts have gained so much prestige and airtime, whose immense public persona seems to speak for millions of others but who (you suspect) actually participates in a 3000-year tradition of ripping them off? You have a short story that needs written and sold to a top tier publication. You've got the concept sketched out; you just need Mr Ai to provide the substance of it, otherwise it'll stall at this, the notes of a writer planning a story about a (scam)artist who may or may not be Ai Weiwei.

At this stage you're ready to call your piece *There is no Ai Weiwei*.

You find yourself back at the start of the exhibit, by the ticket booth with the $45 catalogues. There's a final piece, a full-length mirror titled simply *Ai Weiwei 2022*.